The Pleasure of my Company

The Pleasure of my Company

Steve Martin

W F HOWES LTD

This large print edition published in 2003 by
W F Howes Ltd
Units 6/7, Victoria Mills, Fowke Street
Rothley, Leicester LE7 7PJ

1 3 5 7 9 10 8 6 4 2

First published in the United Kingdom in 2003
by Weidenfeld & Nicolson

A CIP catalogue record for this book is available
from the British Library

ISBN 1 84505 642 6

Typeset by Palimpsest Book Production Limited,
Polmont, Stirlingshire
Printed and bound in Great Britain
by Antony Rowe Ltd, Chippenham, Wilts.

To my mother and father

If I can get from here to the pillar box
If I can get from here to the lamp-post
If I can get from here to the front gate
before a car comes round the corner . . .
  Carolyn Murray will come to tea
  Carolyn Murray will love me too
  Carolyn Murray will marry me
  But only if I get from here to there
before a car comes round the corner . . .

—MICK GOWAR, FROM *OXFORD'S ONE HUNDRED*
  YEARS OF POETRY FOR CHILDREN

The Pleasure of my Company

This all started because of a clerical error. Without the clerical error, I wouldn't have been thinking this way at all; I wouldn't have had time. I would have been too preoccupied with the new friends I was planning to make at Mensa, the international society of geniuses. I'd taken their IQ test, but my score came back missing a digit. Where was the 1 that should have been in front of the 90? I fell short of genius category by a full fifty points, barely enough to qualify me to sharpen their pencils. Thus I was rejected from membership and facing a hopeless pile of red tape to correct the mistake.

This clerical error changed my plans for a while and left me with a few idle hours I hadn't counted on. My window to the street consumed a lot of them. Nice view: I can see the Pacific Ocean, though I have to lean out pretty far, almost to my heels. Across the street is a row of exotically named apartment buildings, which provide me with an unending parade of human vignettes. My building, the Chrysanthemum, houses mostly young people, who don't appear to be out of work but are. People

1

in their forties seem to prefer the Rose Crest. Couples whose children are grown gravitate toward the Tudor Gardens, and the elderly flock to the Ocean Point. In other words, a person can live his entire life here and never move from the block.

I saw Elizabeth the other day. What a pleasure! She didn't see me, though; she doesn't know me. But there was a time when Liz Taylor and Richard Burton had never met, yet it doesn't mean they weren't, in some metaphysical place, already in love. Elizabeth was pounding a FOR LEASE sign into the flower bed of the Rose Crest. Her phone number was written right below her name, Elizabeth Warner. I copied it down and went to the gas station to call her, but the recorded voice told me to push so many buttons I just gave up. Not that I couldn't have done it, it was just a complication I didn't need. I waved to Elizabeth once from my window, but maybe there was a reflection or something, because she didn't respond. I went out the next day at the same hour and looked at my apartment, and sure enough, I couldn't see a thing inside, even though I had dressed a standing lamp in one of my shirts and posed it in front of the window.

I was able to cross the street because just a few yards down from my apartment, two scooped-out driveways sit opposite each other. I find it diffi-cult – okay, impossible – to cross the street at the corners. The symmetry of two scooped-out drive-ways facing each other makes a lot of sense to me.

I see other people crossing the street at the kerb and I don't know how they can do it. Isn't a kerb forbidding? An illogical elevation imposing itself between the street and the sidewalk? Crosswalks make so much sense, but laid between two ominous kerbs they might as well be at the bottom of the Mariana Trench. Who designed this? Daffy Duck?

You are now thinking I'm either brilliant or a murder suspect. Why not both? I'm teasing you. I am a murder suspect, but in a very relaxed way and definitely not guilty. I was cleared way early, but I'm still a suspect. Head spinning? Let me explain. Eight months ago a neighbor downstairs, Bob the appliance repairman, was knifed dead. Police came to interview me – it was just routine – and Officer Ken saw a bloodstained parka on my coatrack. Subsequently the lab found fibers from my parka on the corpse. Can you figure out my alibi? Take a minute.

Here it is: One night a naked woman burst out of Bob the appliance repairman's apartment, hysterical. I grabbed my parka and threw it around her. Bob came and got her, but he was so polite he made me suspicious. Too bad I didn't get fully suspicious until a week later, just after naked woman had penetrated his liver with a kitchen knife. One day, the naked woman, now dressed, returned my parka, unaware that blood and other damning evidence stained the backside. I was unaware too until savvy cop spotted the blood-stain when the parka was hanging on a coat hook

3

near the kitchen. The cops checked out my story and it made sense; Amanda, hysterical woman, was arrested. End of story.

Almost. I'm still a suspect, though not in the conventional sense. My few moments of infamy are currently being reenacted because the producers of *Crime Show*, a TV documentary program that recreates actual murders, love the bloodstained parka angle, so I'm being thrown in as a red herring. They told me to just 'act like myself.' When I said, 'How do I do that?' they said to just have fun with it, but I'm not sure what they meant.

I'm hoping that my status as a murder suspect will enhance my first meeting with Elizabeth. It could jazz things up a bit. Of course, in the same breath I will tell her that I was cleared long ago, but I'll wait just that extra second before I do in order to make sure I've enchanted her.

The larger issue, the one that sends me to the dictionary of philosophy, if I had one, is the idea of acting like myself. Where do my hands go when I'm myself? Are they in my pockets? I frankly can't remember. I have a tough time just *being* myself, you know, at parties and such. I start talking to someone and suddenly I know I am no longer myself, that some other self has taken over.

The less active the body, the more active the mind. I had been sitting for days, and my mind made this curious excursion into a tangential problem: Let's say my shopping list consists of two items: Soy sauce and talcum powder. Soy sauce and talcum powder could not be more dissimilar. Soy: tart and salty. Talc: smooth and silky. Yet soy sauce and talcum powder are both available at the same store, the grocery store. Airplanes and automobiles, however, are similar. Yet if you went to a car lot and said, 'These are nice, but do you have any airplanes?' they would look at you like you're crazy.

So here's my point. This question I'm flipping around – what it means to act like myself – is related to the soy sauce issue. Soy and talc are mutually exclusive. Soy is not talc and vice versa. I am not someone else, someone else is not me. Yet we're available in the same store. The store of Existence. This is how I think, which vividly illustrates Mensa's loss.

Thinking too much also creates the illusion of causal connections between unrelated events. Like the morning the toaster popped up just as a car drove by with Arizona plates. Connection? Or coincidence? Must the toaster be engaged in order for a car with Arizona plates to come by? The problem, of course, is that I tend to behave as if these connections were real, and if a car drives by with plates from, say, Nebraska, I immediately eyeball the refrigerator to see if its door has swung open.

I stay home a lot because I'm flush with cash right now ($600 in the bank, next month's rent already paid), so there's no real need to seek work. Anyway, seeking work is a tad difficult given the

5

poor design of the streets with their prohibitive curbs and driveways that don't quite line up. To get to the Rite Aid, the impressively well-stocked drugstore that is an arsenal of everything from candies to camping tents, I must walk a circuitous maze discovered one summer after several weeks of trial and error. More about the Rite Aid later (Oh God, Zandy – so cute! And what a pharmacist!).

My grandmother (my angel and savior) sends me envelopes periodically from her homestead with cash or cash equivalents that make my life possible. And quite a homestead she has. Think *Tara* squashed and elongated and dipped in adobe. I would love to see her, but a trip to Helmut, Texas, would require me to travel by mass transportation, which is on my list of no-no's. Crowds of four or more are just not manageable for me, unless I can create a matrix that links one individual to another by connecting similar shirt patterns. And airplanes, trains, buses, and cars . . . well, please. I arrived in California twelve years ago when my travel options were still open, but they were quickly closed down due to a series of personal discoveries about enclosed spaces, rubber wheels, and the logic of packing, and there was just no damn way for me to get back home.

You might think not going out would make me lonely, but it doesn't. The natural disorder of an apartment building means that sooner or later everyone, guided by principles of entropy, will inadvertently knock on everyone else's door. Which is how I became the Wheatgrass guy. After the murder, gossip whipped through our hallways like a Fury, and pretty soon everyone was talking to everyone else. Philipa, the smart and perky actress who lives one flight up, gabbed with me while I was half in and half out of my open doorway (she was a suspect too for about a split second because the soon-to-be-dead guy had once offended her in a three-second unwelcome embrace by letting his hand slip lower than it properly should have, and she let everyone know she was upset about it). Philipa told me she was nervous about an upcoming TV audition. I said let me make you a wheatgrass juice. I wanted to calm her down so she could do her best. She came into my apartment and I blended a few herbs in a tall glass. Then, as a helpful afterthought, I broke an Inderal in half, which I carried in my pocket pillbox, and mixed it into the drink. Inderal is a heart medication, intended to straighten out harmless arrhythmias, which I sometimes get, but has a side effect of leveling out stage fright, too. Well, Philipa reported later that she gave the best audition of her life and got two callbacks. Probably no connection to the Inderal-laced drink, but maybe. The point is she wanted to believe in the wheatgrass juice, and she started coming back for more at regular intervals. She would stop by and take a swig, sit a while and talk about her actress-y things, and then leave for her next audition with a tiny dose of a drug that was blocking her betas.

If the moon is out of orbit one inch a year, eventually, somewhere in a future too distant to imagine, it will spin out of control and smash into, say, India. So comparatively speaking, a half an Inderal in a wheatgrass juice once or twice a week for Philipa is not really a problem, but if I'm to stay in orbit with Philipa, my own prescription count needs to be upped. Easy for me, as all I have to do is exaggerate my condition to the doctor at the Free Clinic and more pills are on the way. My real dilemma began one afternoon when Philipa complained that she was not sleeping well. Did I have a juice drink that might help? she asked. I couldn't say no to her because she had grown on me. Not in the way of Elizabeth the Realtor, who had become an object of desire, but in the way of a nice girl up the stairs whose adventures kept me tuned in like a soap opera.

Philipa couldn't see that she was in the charmed part of her life when hope woke her up every day and put her feet into her shoes. She lived with a solid, but in my view, dimwit guy, who would no doubt soon disappear and be replaced by a sharper banana. I went to the kitchen and blended some orange juice, protein powder, a plum, and a squirt of liquid St John's Wort from the Rite Aid, and then, confidently motivated by poor judgment, I dropped in one-quarter of a Quaalude.

These Quaaludes were left over from a college party and had hung out in my kitchen drawer ever since, still in their original package. I didn't even know if they were still potent, but they seemed to work for Philipa, because about ten minutes after she drank my elixir, a dreamy smile came over her face and she relaxed into my easy chair and told me her entire history with the current boyfriend, whose name was Brian. She commented on his hulking, glorious penis, which was at first phrased as '. . . great dick . . .' – Philipa had begun to slur – and then later, when she began to slur more poetically, was described as a 'uniform shaft with a slight parenthetical bend.' Evidently it had captivated her for months until one day it stopped captivating her. Brian still assumed it was the center of their relationship, and Philipa felt obligated to continue with him because her fixation on his failsafe penis had drawn him into her nest in the first place. But now this weighty thing remained to be dealt with, though Philipa's interest had begun to flag.

The Quaalude drink became first a monthly ritual, then bi-weekly, then bidiurnal, and then I started hiding every night around 11 P.M. when she would knock on my door. My supply of the secret ingredient was getting low, and I was glad, because I was beginning to doubt the morality of the whole enterprise. She did say one night, as she waited for the plum/orange elixir to take effect, that the drink had rekindled her interest in Brian's thing and that she loved to lie there while he did things to her. In fact, that's the way she liked it now, her eyelids at half-mast and Brian at full.

When I started to cut back on the amount of the drug, for reasons of conscience as well as supply, her interest in him waned and I could tell that Brian was on his way out again. For a while, by varying the dose, I could orchestrate their relationship like a conductor, but when I finally felt bad enough, I cut her off without her ever knowing she'd been on it and seemingly with no deleterious effects. Somehow, their relationship hung together.

Santa Monica, California, where I live, is a perfect town for invalids, homosexuals, show people, and all other formerly peripheral members of society. Average is not the norm here. Here, if you're visiting from Omaha, you stick out like a senorita's ass at the Puerto Rican day parade. That's why, when I saw a contest at the Rite Aid drugstore (eight blocks from my house, takes me forty-seven minutes to get there) asking for a two-page essay on why I am the most average American, I marveled that the promoters actually thought that they might find an average American at this nuthouse by the beach. This cardboard stand carried an ad by its sponsor, Tepperton's Frozen Apple Pies. I grabbed an entry form, and as I hurried home (thirty-five minutes: a record), began composing the essay in my head.

The challenge was not how to present myself as average, but how to make myself likable without lying. I think I'm pretty appealing, but likability in an essay is very different from likability in life. See, I tend to grow on people, and five hundred words is just not enough to get someone to like me. I need several years and a ream or two of paper. I knew I had to flatter, overdo, and lay it on thick in order to speed up my likability time frame. So I would not like the sniveling, patriotic me who wrote my five hundred words. I would like a girl with dark roots peeking out through the peroxide who was laughing so hard that Coca-Cola was coming out of her nose. And I guess you would too. But Miss Coca-Cola Nose wouldn't be writing this essay in her Coca-Cola persona. She would straighten up, fix her hair, snap her panties out of her ass, and start typing.

'I am average because . . .,' I wrote, 'I stand on the seashore here in Santa Monica and I let the Pacific Ocean touch my toes, and I know I am at the most western edge of our nation, and that I am a descendant of the settlers who came to California as pioneers. And is not every American a pioneer? Does this spirit not reside in each one of us, in every city, in every heart on every rural road, in every traveler in every Winnebago, in every American living in every mansion or slum? I am average,' I wrote, 'because the cry of individuality flows confidently through my blood, with little attention drawn to itself, like the still power of an apple pie sitting in an open window to cool.'

I hope the Mensa people never see this essay, not because it reeks of my manipulation of a poor company just trying to sell pies, but because, during the twenty-four hours it took me to write it, I believed so fervently in its every word.

Tuesdays and Fridays are big days for me. At least at 2 P.M. At 2 P.M. Clarissa comes. She talks to me for exactly forty-five minutes, but she's not a full shrink; she's a student shrink. So officially she's a visitor and her eyes are green. She brings a little gift bag each time, sometimes with packaged muffins, or phone cards, all of which I assume are donated. She asks me how I am, and she always remembers something from last time that she can follow up on this time. If I told her that I planned to call my mother with the new phone card, she remembers to ask how the call went. Problematic for me, because when I say I'm going to call my mother I am lying, as my mother has been dead – is it six years now? Problematic for her, because Clarissa knows my mother is dead and feels she has to humor me. I know I'm lying and not fooling her, and she thinks I'm crazy and fooling myself. I like this little fib because it connects us at a much deeper level than hello.

Clarissa makes several other stops on Tuesdays and Fridays to other psychiatric charity cases, which I'm sure have earned her several school credits. I was, it seems, one of the low men on the totem pole of insanity and therefore the recipient of treatment from a beginner. This I have scoped out one data bit at a time. When someone doesn't want to give you information about themselves, the only way to acquire it is by reverse inquiry. Ask the questions you don't want answered and start paring away to the truth. My conclusion about her was hard to reach because she's *at least* thirty-three. And still a student? Where were the missing years?

She's probably reporting on me to a professor or writing about me in a journal. I like to think of her scrawling my name in pencil at the end of our sessions – I mean visits – but really, I'm probably a keyboard macro by now. She types *D* and hits control/spacebar and Daniel Pecan Cambridge appears. When she looks me in the face on Tuesdays and Fridays she probably thinks of me not as Daniel Pecan Cambridge but as D-control/spacebar. I, however, think of her only as Clarissa because her movements, gestures, and expressions translate only into the single word of her name.

Last Tuesday: Clarissa arrived in her frisky lip-gloss pink Dodge Neon. She parked on the street, and lucky for both of us, there's a two-hour parking zone extending for several blocks in front of my apartment. So of course she's never gotten a ticket. From my window I saw her waiting by her car talking on the cell phone; I watched her halt mid-street for a car to pass, and I saw its hotshot driver craning his neck to see her in his rearview mirror. She was wearing a knee-length skirt that moved like a bell when she walked. Clarissa has a student quality that I suspect she'll have her whole life.

13

She's definitely the cutest girl in class, and any romantically inclined guy looking for an experiment in cleanliness would zero in on her. Her hair is auburn – do we still use that word? – it looks dark blonde in the Santa Monica sun, but it flickers between red and brown once she's in the apartment. And as Clarissa's hair color is on a sliding scale depending on light and time of day, so is her beauty, which slides on a gradient between normal and ethereal.

She was already focused on me and she set her things down without even looking where she was dumping them. 'Sorry I'm late,' she said. I said, 'You're not.' 'Well, almost,' she added.

I didn't say anything about her apologizing for being *almost* late. I couldn't quite wrap my head around the concept even. If you're almost late, it means you're not late, so what are we talking about?

The thing I like about Clarissa is that she starts talking immediately, which gives me the opportunity to watch her without saying anything.

'You won't believe what happened to me. Yesterday I had a return flight from San Francisco. I really wanted to leave at eight but could only get the reduced fare on the five o'clock. I get to the airport and the five o'clock is canceled, and they've put us on the eight o'clock flight and charged us the full fare! But now my car's parked at Burbank and the eight o'clock goes to LAX, so now I have to pay for a taxi to get me to my car. AND I lost three extra hours in San Francisco.'

It seems as though little ills like this are always befalling Clarissa, which makes her seem younger than she actually is. Once she lost her passport right before a trip to Mexico. Once her cell phone battery went dead at the same time as her car battery. But if Clarissa is hapless, it is not the definition of her. Because I see something that describes her more clearly. It occurs in the pauses in her speech when her eyes fix on an air spot roughly waist-high and she seems to be in a trance. And then suddenly it's as if her mind races, trying to catch up to real time, and she continues right where she left off.

If you saw her in these moments, you might think she was collecting her thoughts in order to go forward. But I see it another way: Her mind is being overwhelmed by two processes that must simultaneously proceed at full steam. One is to deal with and live in the present world. The other is to re-experience and mourn something that happened long ago. It is as though her lightness pulls her toward heaven, but the extra gravity around her keeps her earthbound.

Or is it that I think too much?

My redress with the Mensa people is going well. Here's the progress so far: I am thinking of writing a letter asking them to rescore my test. My potential inquiry could be embarrassing for them. They would be compelled to look harder at my results and install me as a full Mensa member, with

15

apologia, if there is such a category. Right now, there's not much more I can do other than wait for me to write the letter.

I don't know if I want to approach Elizabeth the Realtor until the Mensa thing is worked out. My membership would be nice to drop over drinks on our third date. If I get the feeling there might not be a third date, I have no qualms about moving it up to our second date, or even blurting it out on our first date right after 'hello.' I am thinking about her because I spotted her twice today, once going and once coming. The apartments across the street are not easy to rent, lucky for me, and therefore numerous showings are required in order to find the one customer who is willing to pay top dollar for the mediocre. When she pulled up in front of the Rose Crest, every one of my senses went on alert. I slid open the window, and I swear the scent of lilac or lavender wafted toward me even though she was at least a hundred feet away. The aroma was so heavy I tasted it on my tongue. I gripped the windowsill, burying my fingers in the aluminum groove. I saw her angle herself out of her diesel Mercedes with the practiced perfection of a beauty queen. I heard her shoes hit the asphalt with a clap.

She went into the building, never moving her cell phone from her ear, and twenty minutes later I saw a couple in their thirties, Porsche-equipped, pull up and park half in the red zone. Oh, I can read them like a book: too much money in the

Porsche, not enough left over for the rent. This is a young hotshot three years into his first good job, and the one thing he wants is a Porsche. Sort of the boyhood dream thing. Finally he gets the car and has a strong attachment to it. The wife came later, but dang, he still loves his Porsche. So they think they have plenty of money for rent until they start checking into prices and find that their affordable number of bedrooms had shrunk by 1.5.

I could imagine myself living with Elizabeth. Panty hose at breakfast, high heels before lunch. I wonder if the age difference is a problem? She must be forty-two. I must be, say, thirty-five. (Of course, I know my own age, and I have no qualms about mentioning it. It's just that I would act older than I am if I were with Elizabeth, and I would act younger than I am if I were with Zandy the pharmacist.) I doubt that Elizabeth would want to live here in my place. I assume she lives in some fine rental property, the choicest out of the hundreds she must handle daily, and gotten at a bargain price. So obviously *I* would be moving in with *her*. But would she be tolerant when I started listing my peculiarities? Would she understand my need for the apartment's lightbulbs to total exactly 1125 watts when lit?

I sat waiting at my window for Elizabeth to reemerge, my eyes shifting from her car to the apartment's security gate and back again. The thing about a new romance like this is that previously explainable things become inexplicable when juiced with the fury of love. Which led me to believe, when I saw the trunk of her car mysteriously unlatch and the lid slowly yawn open, that it was caused by the magnetic forces of our attraction to each other. Now, looking back, I realize it was a radar feature on her car key that enabled her to open the trunk from forty feet, when she was just out of my sight line. When she got to her car, she reached in the trunk and handed her clients two brochures that I suppose were neatly stacked next to the spare tire.

They stood and chatted curbside, and I saw that this wasn't a perfunctory handshake and good-bye; she was still pitching and discussing the apart-ment. This was my opportunity to meet my *object d'amour*. Or at least give her the chance to see me, to get used to me. My plan was to walk by on my side of the street and not look over her way. This, I felt, was a very clever masculine move: to meet and ultimately seduce through *no contact at all*. She would be made aware of me as a mysterious figure, someone with no need of her whatsoever. This is compelling to a woman.

When I hit the street, I encountered a problem. I had forgotten to wear sunglasses. So as I walked by her, facing west into the sun, while I may have been an aloof figure, I was an aloof figure who squinted. One half of my face was shut like a salted snail, while the other half was held open in an attempt to see. Just at the moment Elizabeth looked over (I intentionally scuffled my foot, an impetuous

18

betrayal of my own plan to let her notice me on her own), I was half puckered and probably dangerous-looking. My plan required me to keep walking at least around the corner so that she wouldn't find out I had no actual destination. I continued around the block, and with my back now to the sun, I was able to swagger confidently, even though it was pointless as I was well out of her sight. Ten minutes later I came round again. To my dismay, Elizabeth and her clients were still there, and I would again be walking into the 4 P.M. direct sun. This time I forced both my eyes open, which caused them to burn and water. The will required to do this undermined my outward pose of confidence. My walk conveyed the demeanor of a gentleman musketeer, but my face expressed a lifetime of constipation.

Still, as freakish as I may have appeared, I had established contact. And I doubt that her brief distorted impression of me was so indelible that it could not, at some point, be erased and replaced with a better me.

Which leads me to the subject of charisma. Wouldn't we all like to know the extent of our own magnetism? I can't say my charm was at full throttle when I strolled by Elizabeth, but had she been at the other end of the street, so that I was walking eastward with the sun behind me, squintless and relaxed and perhaps in dusky silhouette, my own charisma would have swirled out of me like smoke from a hookah. And Elizabeth, the enthralling

Elizabeth, would already be snared and corralled. But my charisma has yet to fully bloom. It's as though something is keeping me back from it. Perhaps fear: What would happen to me and to those around me if my power became uncontained? If I were suddenly just too sensational to be managed? Maybe my obsessions are there to keep me from being too powerfully alluring, to keep my wouldbe lovers and adventures in check. After all, I can't be too seductive if I have to spend a half hour on the big night calculating and adjusting the aggregate bulb wattage in a woman's apartment while she sits on the edge of the bed checking her watch.

Around this time the *Crime Show* called, wanting to tape more footage for their show. They needed to get a long shot of me acting suspicious while I was being interrogated by two policemen who were in fact actors. I asked them what I should say, and they said it didn't matter as the camera would be so far away we would only have to move our mouths to make it look like we're talking. I said okay, because as nervous as it made me, the taping gave the coming week a highlight. The idleness of my life at that time, the unintended vacation I was on, made the days long and the nights extended, though it was easy for me to fill the warm California hours by sitting at the window, adjusting the breeze by using the sliding glass as a louver and watching the traffic roll by.

★　★　★

Eight days after my last sighting of her, I again saw Elizabeth standing across the street, this time with a different couple but doing the same routine. She stood at the car, handing over the brochures, and then dallied as she made her final sales pitch. I decided to take my walk again, this time wearing my sunglasses to avoid the prune look. I outdid myself in the clothes department, too. I put on my best outfit, only realizing later that Elizabeth had no way of knowing that it was my best outfit. She could have thought it was my third- or fourth-best outfit, or that I have a closet full of better outfits of which this was the worst. So although I was actually trying very hard, Elizabeth would have to scour my closet, comparing one outfit against another, in order to realize it. This outfit, so you know, consisted of khaki slacks and a fashionably frayed white dress shirt. I topped it off with some very nice brown loafers and matching socks. This is the perfect ensemble for my neighborhood, by the way. I looked like a Californian, a Santa Monican, a man of leisure.

I attained the sidewalk. I decided this time not to look like someone with a destination but to go for the look of 'a man taking his dog for a walk.' Though I had no dog. But I imagined a leash in my hand; this was so vivid to me I paused a few times to let the invisible dog sniff the occasional visible bush. Such was the depth of my immersion in my 'walking man' character. This time full eye contact was made with Elizabeth, but it was the kind where even though her eyes strayed over toward me, she kept on talking to her clients, in much the same way one would glance over to someone wearing a giant spongy orange fish hat: You want to look, but you don't want to engage.

A plan began to form. As I passed her, I noticed the two opposing driveways coming up, which meant I could cross the street if I wanted and end up on her block. In order to walk near Elizabeth, I would have to reverse my direction once I had crossed the street. But it seemed perfectly natural to me that a man would walk down the street, decide to cross it, then go back and read the realtor sign before going on. This required a little acting on my part. I came to the low scoop of the driveway and even walked a little past it. I paused, I deliberated, I turned and looked back at the sign, which was about a dozen feet from where Elizabeth was standing. I squinted at it, as if it were too far away to see, and proceeded to cross the street and head in Elizabeth's direction.

She was facing away from me; the sign was behind her and stuck into the flower bed, which was really more of a fern bed. She was wearing a tight beige-and-white paisley skirt, and a short sleeve brown blouse that was bursting from within because of her cannonball breasts. Her hair was combed back over her head and held in place by a black velour hair clamp, which fit like headphones. Her feet were plugged into two open-toed patent leather heels and were reflected in the chrome of her

Mercedes' bumper. I couldn't imagine any man to whom this package would not appeal.

As I approached her, I felt a twinge where it matters. And if my theory is correct, that sexual attraction is usually mutual – an evolutionary necessity, otherwise nobody would be doing it with anybody – then Elizabeth must have been feeling something, too. That is, if she ever looked over at me. I came to the sign, leaned over, and pretended to read the description of the apartment, which was reduced to such extreme abbreviations as to be indecipherable. What's a rfna? I had to do mental somersaults to align the fact that while I was reading Elizabeth's name, her actual person was by now two steps behind me.

I stepped backward as if to get a better view of the sign and, I swear this was an accident, bumped right into Elizabeth, glute to glute. She turned her head and said airily, 'I'm sorry,' even though it was I who had bumped into her. 'Oh, excuse *me*,' I said, taking all the blame.

'Are you the realtor?' I asked.

'Yes I am,' she said and she browsed inside her purse without ever losing eye contact with me.

'How many apartments are there for rent in the entire complex of apartments?' I said, using too many words.

'Just three. Would you like a card?'

Oh yes, I wanted a card. I took it, palming it like an ace of spades, knowing it was a memento that I would pin up on my bulletin board. In fact, this would be the first item on the board that could even come close to being called a bulletin. 'That's you,' I said, indicating with a gesture that the name on the card and the name on the sign were one and the same.

'Are you looking for an apartment?' she asked.

I said something exquisite: 'I'm always looking to upgrade.' I muttered this casually as I sauntered off. The wrong way, I might add. The next opposing scooped-out driveways were so far out of my way that I didn't get home for twenty-five minutes, and while I walked I kept looking back over my shoulder at my apartment, which had begun to recede into a pinpoint.

Once home I reflected on the encounter, and two moments in particular stood out. One was Elizabeth's response to my inquiry about the number of apartments for rent. 'Just three.' It was the 'just' I admired. 'Just a few left,' 'Only three and they're going fast' was the implication. Elizabeth was obviously a clever saleswoman. I figured that three were a lot of empty apartments for this building, and that the pressure was on from the owners to get them rented fast. I'll bet they knew what they had in Elizabeth: the very, very best.

The second moment – contact between me and Elizabeth – was harder to relive because it had occurred out of my sight, actually behind my back. So I had to picture the unseen. Our – pardon my language – butts had backed right into each other like two marshmallows coming together in a sudden splat. Boing. If I had intended this sort of physical encounter I would be a different kind of person. The kind I am actually not. I would never do such a thing intentionally, like a subway creep. But I had literally impressed myself upon Elizabeth, and at our next meeting we would be further along than I ever could have imagined, now that she and I had had intimate contact. My hip had touched hers and hers had touched mine. That's probably more than a lot of men have done who have known her a lot longer.

My third contact with Elizabeth, which occurred one week later, was a total failure, with an explanation. I was coincidentally on the street when Elizabeth pulled up and got out of her car. Nothing could have seemed more casual, more unplanned, than my presence in front of the Rose Crest. She unfolded herself from the Mercedes, all legs and stockings, and gave me a jaunty wave. I think she was even about to speak to me. The problem was, I was taping my long shot for the *Crime Show*, in which I was supposedly being interrogated by two cops on the street.

So when Elizabeth waved, I was approached by two 'policemen' who seriously overacted in their efforts to make me look guilty by snarling and poking at me. Luckily it was a long shot, so their hambone performances couldn't be seen on camera. No Emmy for them. I thought I was pretty good. We were given no dialogue to say, but we had been asked to spout gibberish while a narrator talked over us. They weren't recording us, they just wanted our mouths to be moving to make it look like we were talking. One 'policeman' was saying, 'I'm talking, I'm talking, I'm moving my mouth, it looks like I'm talking.' And then the other one would say, 'Now I'm talking, I'm moving my mouth like I'm talking.' Then they would say to me, 'Now you talk, just move your mouth.' So I would say, 'I'm talking, I'm talking, I'm talking back to you,' and so on. I couldn't wave to Elizabeth, even though she'd waved at me, as it would have spoiled the scene. I must have looked strange, because even though it was eighty-five-degree weather, I was wearing the blue parka with the bloodstain to look even more suspicious for the camera. This couldn't have made Elizabeth too comfortable, particularly if she'd had any inclination toward viewing me as her next husband.

I am always amazed by what lies buried in the mind until one day for no particular reason it rises up and makes itself known. That night in bed, a vision of Elizabeth's face entered my consciousness, and I saw clearly that she had gray-green eyes. It was a small fact I hadn't realized I knew.

On Sunday I decided to distract myself by going down to the Rite Aid and taking a look at Zandy. This was no ordinary girl watching. Zandy works at the pharmacy, behind an elevated counter. She's visible only from the neck up as she sails from one end to the other. If I visit the pay phone/Coke machine alcove, I can get an employee's view of Zandy's pharmacy-white outfit against her pharmacy-white skin. She's a natural California girl, except her face has never been touched by makeup or sun, only by the flourescent rays of the ceiling lights. Her hair is almost unkempt, with so many dangling swoops and curls that I long for a tiny surfboard so I can go swishing amid the tresses. I have no designs on Zandy because the rejection would be overwhelming for me. Plus, she's a genuine blonde, and I prefer Elizabeth's dyed look.

The Rite Aid is splendidly antiseptic. I'll bet the floors are hosed down every night with isopropyl alcohol. The Rite Aid is the axle around which my squeaky world turns, and I find myself there two or three days a week seeking out the rare household item such as cheesecloth. Like every other drugstore on earth, it is filled with quack products that remind me of nineteenth-century ads for hair restorers and innervating elixirs. These days there is a solid percentage of products in the stores which actually work, but they're on display next to liquid-filled shoe inserts that claim to prevent varicose veins.

I pretended to stop for a Coke 'n' phone – even though my phone card was on empty – and saw Zandy gliding behind the counter, as though she were on skates. I moved to the end of the displays, pretending to read the instructions for the Coke machine, and good news, the wonderful minds at the Rite Aid had decided to move the Tepperton's Apple Pie Most Average American essay contest placard next to the Coke machine, where I could tear off an entry form and, for the next few minutes, write another five hundred words while Zandy, delicious as a meringue, went about her work in full view. I did not really want to write another five hundred words or even two hundred words, but it was easy enough considering the trade-off. There were several dull pencils in a box on the display, so dull that when I wrote with them the wood scraped against the paper, but I buckled down and began my second patriotic essay in two weeks, after a lifetime of none.

America lets me choose not to be a pioneer. I am uplifted by doing ordinary work. The work of society, the common work of the world . . .

And so it went. I was impressed with myself because this essay expressed the exact opposite idea of my first essay – one week I said I had the pioneer spirit and the next week I didn't – and I wrote both opinions with such ease that I believed I could take any subject and effectively argue either side. This skill would be valuable in dating. Just think, I could switch positions midstream if I sensed my date reacting badly.

While I was writing, I barely looked up at Zandy, since I'd realized what a foolish enterprise this was anyway. There is no pleasure in staking out a woman and eyeing her endlessly. I get no more joy from looking at a Monet for twenty minutes than I do after five. A glimpse of Zandy was all that was necessary, and perhaps I used her as an excuse to get out of the house. I signed this second essay using a pseudonym – Lenny Burns – and dropped it in the bin. I bought some foam earplugs (not that I needed them, but at two dollars a dozen, they were too cheap to pass up) and went home.

My ceiling is not conducive to counting. Its texture is created by pulling the trowel flatly away from the wet plaster, leaving a rippled surface, as though a baker had come in and spread around vanilla icing with a spatula. Counting prefers symmetry of some kind, though at my level of sophistication I can get around most obstacles. The least interesting ceiling for me now is one that is practically counted out already: squared-off acoustical tiles with regular punctures that simply require a little multiplication on my part. Each tile has sixty-four sound-absorbing holes times the easily calculated number of tiles in the ceiling. Ugh.

But my irregular ceiling – no tiles, no quadrants, no recurring punctures – takes a little thought on my part to slice up, count, and quantify. Like an ocean, its surface is irregular, but also like an ocean it's easy to imagine an unbroken plane just below the surface of the undulating waves. Once I can imagine an unbroken plane, the bisecting and trisecting of my fairly square ceiling becomes much easier. Triangles, rectangles, and interlocking parallelograms are all superimposed over the ceiling, and in my mind they meld into the birthday-cake frosting of the plaster.

The problem with counting is that anything, any plane, any object, can be divided infinitely, like the distance covered by Zeno's tortoise heading for the finish line. So it's a problem knowing when to stop. If I've divided my ceiling into sixty-four sections (sometimes irregular sections just to annoy myself), I wonder whether to halve it again and again and again. But that's not all. The sections must be sliced up in three-dimensional space, too, so the numbers become unmanageable very quickly. But that's the thing about a brain: Plenty of room for large numbers.

Sure, I've gotten some disbelieving stares when I've tried to explain this little habit of mine to, say, a bus seatmate. I've watched a guy adjust his posture, or get up and move back several rows, even if it meant he now sat next to someone else who was clearly on the verge of some other kind of insanity. You should know, however, that my habit of counting began early – I can't remember if I was a teen or bubbling under at age twelve. My mother was driving up Lone Star Avenue and I was in the backseat. A gasoline truck pulled up next to us at a stoplight and I became fixated on its giant tires. I noticed that even though the tires were round, they still had four points: north, south, east, and west. And when the light changed and the truck started rolling, the north, south, east, and west points of the tire remained constant, that the tire essentially rolled right through them. This gave me immeasurable satisfaction. When the next truck came by, I watched the tires rotate while its polar quadrants remained fixed. Soon, this tendency became a habit, then a compulsion. Eventually the habit compounded and not only tires, but vases, plates, lawns, and living rooms were dissected and strung with imaginary grids.

I can remember only one incident of this habit prior to my teen years. Eight years old, I sat with my parents in our darkened living room watching TV. My father muttered something to me, and my response was slow. Perhaps intentionally slow. I replied disinterestedly, 'Huh?' with hardly enough breath to make it audible. My father's fist uppercut the underside of his dinner tray, sending it flying, and he rose and turned toward me, whipping his belt from his waist. My mind froze him in action and I saw, like ice cracking, a bifurcating line run from his head to his feet. Next, a horizontal line split him at midpoint, then the rest of the lines appeared, dividing him into eighths, sixteenths, thirty-seconds, and so on. I don't remember what happened next.

My counting habit continued into college, where its real import, purpose, and power were revealed to me. The class assignments seemed trifling, but the irresistible counting work seemed vital not only to my well-being but to the world's. I added textbook page numbers together, divided them by the total page numbers, and using my own formulas, redistributed them more appropriately. Page 262 of *Science and Environment* could become a more natural page 118, and I would razor-cut the leaves from their binding and rearrange them to suit my calculations. I had to read them in their new order, too, which made study difficult, and then finally, as I added new rules and limitations to my study habits, impossible. Eventually my quirks were picked up by various professors and savvy teaching assistants, and they, essentially, 'sent me to the nurse.' After a few days of testing, I was urged out of school. I then went to Hewlett-Packard, where I landed a job as a business communiqué encoder.

One time, when I was working at Hewlett-Packard, I tried medication, but it made me uneasy. It was as though the drug were keeping me from the true purpose of each day, which was to count loci and accommodate variables. I slowly took myself off the pills and eventually I left my encoding job. Or maybe it left me. When the chemicals let go of my mind, I could no longer allow myself to create a code when I knew all along that its ultimate end was to be decoded. But that's what the job was, and I couldn't get the bosses to see it my way. Finally, the government began providing me with free services and one of them was Clarissa.

★　★　★

Clarissa the shrink-in-training clinked three times on my door with her Coke can. The knock of someone whose hands are full. The door opened on its own, and I remembered not hearing it latch when I entered earlier with my small sack of earplugs. Clarissa, balancing a cell phone, brief-case, sweater (pointless in today's weather), Palm Pilot, soda can, and wrapped baby gift (she hadn't wanted to leave it in the car), closed the door and made a purse-induced leathery squeak as she crossed the room. I liked her outfit: a maroon skirt topped by a white blouse with a stiffly starched front piece that was vaguely heart-shaped, giving her the appearance of an Armani-clad nurse. (Oh yes, I keep up with the fashions. I noted how close her outfit was to my own favorite: light cotton pants with a finely pressed white dress shirt. No problem, as I love to iron. Once I ironed a pillow almost perfectly flat.) 'Hi,' she said, and 'Hi,' I said back. 'Oh,' she said, 'sorry I'm late.' Of course she wasn't. She just assumed she was late because the traffic had been murder. 'Are you having a good week?' she asked.

I was having a good week, though I couldn't really tell her why. At least, not without her thinking I was obsessed with women. I didn't tell her about my three encounters with Elizabeth, or about eyeballing Zandy at the pharmacy. So I lied and said . . . well, I don't remember what I said. But I do remember a particular moment when, after I'd asked her how she was, she paused that extra second before she said the perfunctory 'fine.' She wasn't fine, and I could tell. I could tell because my mind has the ability to break down moments the way it can break down ceiling tiles. I can cut a moment into quarters, then eighths, then et cetera, and I am able to analyze whether one bit of behavior truly follows another, which it seldom does when a person is disturbed or influenced by a hidden psychic flow.

I couldn't make out what was troubling Clarissa because she's adept at being sunny. I'm going to tell you one of the joys of being Clarissa's 'patient.' While she is analyzing me, I am analyzing her. What makes it fun is that we're both completely unskilled at it. Our conversation that day went like this:

'Did you find a parking space okay?' I asked.

'Oh yes.'

I said they've been hard to find because of the beach-y weather.

'Did you go out this week?' she asked.

'Several walks and a few trips to the Rite Aid.'

'You were fine with it?' she said.

'Yeah. The rules are so easy to follow. Don't you think?'

'I'm not sure what your rules are.'

'I'll bet more people have rules like mine than you think.' I asked, 'What are your rules?' (I wondered if she'd fall for this.)

'Let's stick to you,' she said.

Outwitted!

The conversation went on, with both of us parrying and thrusting. I urged myself to never get well because that would be the end of Clarissa's visits . . . wouldn't it? Though she would probably have to stop one day when she graduates or when her course – meaning me – is over. One of us is getting screwed: Either she's a professional and I should be paying her, or she's an intern and I'm a guinea pig.

Then something exciting happened. Her cell phone rang. It was exciting because what crossed her face ranged wildly on the map of human emotion. And oh, did I divide that moment up into millionths:

The phone rang.

She decided to ignore it.

She decided to answer it.

She decided to ignore it.

She decided to check caller-id.

She looked at the phone display.

She turned off the phone and continued speaking.

But the moment before turning off the phone broke down further into submoments:

She worried that it might be a specific person.

She saw that it was.

She turned off the phone with an angry snap.

But this submoment broke down into even more sub-submoments:

She grieved.

Pain shot through her like a lightning strike.

So, Clarissa had an ex she was still connected to. I said, 'Clarissa, you're a desirable girl; just sit quietly and you will resurrect.' But wait, I didn't say it. I only thought it.

I stayed in my apartment for the next three days. A couple of times Philipa stopped by hoping for more joy juice. I was starting to feel like a pusher and regretted giving her the Mickeys in the first place. But I eased the guilt by reminding myself that the drugs were legal or, in the case of Quaaludes, had at one time been legal. I gave her the plain Jane concoctions of apple and banana, though I wrestled with just telling her the truth and letting her get the drugs herself. But I didn't, because I still enjoyed her stopping by, because I liked her – or is it that I liked her dog? 'Here, Tiger.' When Philipa walked up or down the stairway, so did her dog, and I could hear his four paws ticking and clicking behind her. She'd talk to him as if he were a person, a person who could talk back. Often when she said 'Here, Tiger,' I would say to myself 'No, *here*, Tiger,' hoping doggy ESP would draw him toward my door, because I liked to look into his cartoon face. Tiger was a perfectly assembled mutt, possessing a vocabulary of two dozen words. He had a heart of gold and was keenly alert. He had a variety of quirky mannerisms that could charm a room, such as sleeping on his back while one active hind leg pedaled an invisible bicycle. But his crowning feature was his exceedingly dumb Bozo face, a kind of triangle with eyes, which meant his every act of intelligence was greeted with cheers and praise because one didn't expect such a dimwit to be able to retrieve, and then sort, a bone, a tennis ball, and a rubber dinosaur on verbal commands only. Philipa demonstrated his talent on the lawn one day last summer when she made Tiger go up to apartment 9 and bring down all his belongings and place them in a rubber ring. Philipa's boyfriend, Brian, stood by on the side-lines drinking a Red Bull while shouting 'Dawg, dawg!' And I bet he was also secretly using the dog as a spellchecker.

The view from my window was quite static that weekend. Unfortunately the Sunday *Times* cross-word was a snap (probably to atone for last Sunday's puzzle, which would have stumped the Sphinx), and I finished it in forty-five minutes, including the cryptic, with no mistakes and no erasures. This disrupted my time budget. A couple of cars slowed in front of Elizabeth's realty sign, indicating that she might be showing up later in the week. But the weather was cool and there were no bicyclists, few joggers, no families pouring out of their SUVs and hauling the entire inventory of the Hammacher Schlemmer beach catalogue down to the ocean, so I had no tableaux to write captions for. This slowness made every hour seem like two, which made my idle time problem even worse. I vacuumed, scrubbed the bathroom, cleaned the kitchen. Ironed, ironed, ironed. What did I iron? My shirt, shirt, shirt. At one point I was so bored

I reattached my cable to the TV and watched eight minutes of a Santa Monica city government hearing on mall pavement.

Then it was evening. For a while everything was the same, except now it was dark. Then I heard Brian come down the stairs, presumably in a huff. His walk was an exaggerated stomp meant to send angry messages like African drums. Every footstep boasted 'I don't need her.' No doubt later, in the sports bar, other like-minded guys would agree that Brian was not pussy-whipped, affirmed by the fact that Brian was in the bar watching a game and not outside Philipa's apartment sailing paper airplanes through her window with I LOVE YOU written on them.

Brian strode with a gladiator's pride to his primered '92 Lincoln and split with a gas pedal roar. I then heard someone descending the stairs, who was undoubtedly Philipa. But her pace was not that of a woman in pursuit of her fleeing boyfriend. She was slow-walking in my direction and I could hear the gritty slide of each deliberate footstep. She stopped just outside and lingered an unnaturally long time. Then she rang my doorbell, holding the button down so I heard the *ding*, but not the *dong*.

I pretended to be just waking as I opened the door. Philipa released the doorbell as she swung inside. 'You up?' she asked. 'I'm way up,' I said, dropping my charade of sleep, which I realized was a lie with no purpose. I moved to my armchair (a gift from Granny) and nestled in. Philipa's center-parted hair, long and ash brown, fell straight to her shoulders and framed her pale un-made-up face, and for the first time I could see that this was a pretty girl in the wrong business. She was pretty enough for one man, not for the wide world that show business required. She looked sharp, too; they must have come from an event, had a spat, and now here she was with something on her mind. She sat down on the sofa, stiffened her arms against the armrests, and surprised me by skipping the Brian topic. Instead, her eyes watered up and she said, 'I can't get a job.'

She definitely had had a few drinks. I wondered if she wanted something chemical from me, which I wasn't about to give her, and which I didn't have. 'I thought you just finished a job, that show *The Lawyers*.'

'I did,' she said. 'I played a sandwich girl, delivering lunches to the law office. I was happy to get it. I poured my heart into it. I tried to be a sexy sandwich girl, a memorable sandwich girl, but they asked me to tone it down. So I was just a delivery girl. My line was "Mr Anderson, same as yesterday?" I did it perfectly, too, in one take, and then it was over. I look at the star, Cathy Merlot – can you believe how stupid that name is? Merlot? Why not Susie Cabernet? – and I know I'm as good as she is, but she's the center of attention, she's the one getting fluffed and powder-puffed and . . .'

Philipa kept talking but I stopped listening. By now her body was folded in the chair like an origami stork, her elbows, forearms, calves, and thighs going every which-a-way. She didn't even finish her last sentence; it just trailed off. I think the subject had changed in her head while her mouth had continued on the old topic, not realizing it was out of supplies. She asked me how old I was.

'Thirty-three,' I said. 'I thought you were late twenties,' she said. I explained, 'I never go out in the sun.' She said, 'Must be hard to avoid.' I thought, Oh goody, repartee. But Philipa quieted. It seemed – oddly – that she had become distracted by my presence, the very person she was talking to. Her eyes, previously darting and straying, fell on me and held. She adjusted her body in the sofa and turned her knees squarely toward me, foreshortening her thighs, which disappeared into the shadows of her skirt. This made me uncomfortable and at the same time gave me a hint of an erection.

'When's your birthday?' she asked.

'January twenty-third.'

'You're an Aquarius,' she said.

'I guess. What's yours?' I asked.

'Scorpio.'

'I mean your birth date.'

'November fifteenth.'

I said, 'What year?'

She said, 'Nineteen seventy-four.'

'A Friday,' I said.

'Yes,' she said, not recognizing my sleight of hand. 'Do you date anyone?'

'Oh yeah,' I said. 'I'm dating a realtor.'

'Are you exclusive?'

'No,' I said. 'But she wants me to be.'

Then she paused. Cocked her head like Tiger. 'Wait a minute. How did you know it was a Friday?' she finally asked.

How do I explain to her what I can't explain to myself? 'It's something I can do,' I said.

'What do you mean?'

'I mean I don't know, I can just do it.'

'What's April 8, 1978?'

'It's a Saturday,' I said.

'Jeez, that's freaky. You're right; it's my brother's birthday; he was born on Saturday. What's January 6, 1280?'

'Tuesday,' I said.

'Are you lying?' she asked.

'No.'

'What do you do for a living, and do you have any wine?'

'No wine,' I said, answering one question and skirting the other.

'So you want some wine? I've got some upstairs,' she said. Open, I'll bet, too, I thought. 'Okay,' I said, knowing I wasn't going to have any. Philipa excused herself and ran up to her apartment with a 'be right back.' I stayed in my chair, scratching around the outline of its paisley pattern with my

41

fingernail. Soon she was back with a bottle of red wine. 'Fuck,' she said. 'All I had was Merlot.'

Philipa poured herself a tankard full and slewed around toward me, saying, 'So what did you say you do?'

I wanted to seem as if I were currently employed, so I had to change a few tenses. Mostly 'was' to 'am.' 'I encode corporate messages. Important messages are too easily hacked if sent by computer. So they were looking for low-tech guys to come up with handwritten systems. I developed a system based on the word "floccinaucinihilipilification."' I had lost Philipa. Proof of how boring the truth is. She had bottomed-up the tankard, and I know what wine does. Right now I was probably looking to her like Pierce Brosnan. She stood up and walked toward me, putting both hands on my chair and leaning in. I kept talking about codes. She brushed my cheek with her lips.

I knew what I was to Philipa. A moment. And she was attached to Brian, in spite of the recent storm clouds. And I was attached to Elizabeth even though she didn't know my name. And I knew that if Philipa and I were to seize this moment, the hallway would be forever changed. Every footstep would mean something else. Would she avoid me? Should I avoid her? What would happen if she met Elizabeth? Would Elizabeth know? Women are mind readers in the worst way. But on the other hand, I knew that if I dabbled with Philipa that night, I could be entering the pantheon of historical and notable affairs. There is a grand tradition involving the clandestine. The more I thought about it, the less this seemed like a drunken one-off and more like the stuff of novels. And this perhaps would be my only opportunity to engage in it.

By now, Philipa's eyelashes were brushing my cheek and her breath was on my mouth. With both hands, I clutched the arms of my chair as if I were on a thrill ride. I pooched out my lower lip, and that was all the seduction she needed. She took my hand and led me into my own bedroom. I'm sure that Philipa was lured on by my best asset, which is my Sure-cuts hairdo. I'm lanky like a baseball pitcher, and the Sure-cut people know how to give me the floppy forehead at a nominal price. So without bragging, I'm letting you know that I can be physically appealing. Plus I'm clean. Clean like I've just been car-washed and then scrubbed with a scouring pad and then wrapped in palm fronds infused with ginger. My excellent personal hygiene, in combination with the floppy casual forehead, once resulted in a provocative note being sent to me from my former mailwoman. Philipa never saw females going in and out, so she knew I wasn't a lothario, and I had come to suspect that she regarded me as a standby if she ever needed to get even with Brian the wide receiver.

I never have interfered with a relationship, out of respect for the guy as much as for myself, but Brian is a dope and Philipa is a sylph and I am a man, even if that description of myself is qualified by my failure to be able to cross the street at the curb.

The bedroom was a little too bright for Philipa. She wanted to lower the lights, so I turned out three sixty-watt bulbs but had to go to the kitchen to turn on a one-hundred-watt bulb and a fifty-watt bulb and two fifteens, in order to maintain equity. It is very hard to get thirty-watt bulbs, so when I find them I hoard them.

She still didn't like the ambience. The overhead lights disturbed her. I turned them off and compensated by turning on the overheads in the living room. But the light spilling into the bedroom was just too much; she wanted it dim and sexy. She went over and closed the door. Oh no, the door can't be closed; not without elaborate preparations. Because if the door is closed, the light in the bedroom is cut off from the light in the living room. Rather than having one grand sum of 1125 watts, there would be two discrete calculations that would break the continuity. I explained this to Philipa, even though I had to go through it several times. To her credit, she didn't run, she just got tired, and a little too drunk to move. Our erotic moment had fallen flat, so I walked her to the door. I hadn't succeeded with Philipa, but at least I could still look Elizabeth straight in the eye.

After Philipa left, I lay in the center of the bed with the blanket neatly tucked around me; how Philipa and I would have mussed it! Inserted so neatly between the bed and the sheets, I thought how much I must look like a pocket pencil. My body was so present. I was aware of my toes, my arms, my weight on the bed. There was just me in a void, wrapped in the low hum of existence. The night of Philipa had led me to a quiet, aesthetic stillness. You might think it odd to call a moment of utter motionlessness life, but it was life without interaction, and I felt joy roll over me in a silent wave.

As long as I remained in bed, my relationship to Elizabeth was flawless. I was able to provide for her, to tease out a smile from her, and to keep her supplied with Versace stretch pants. But I knew that during the day, in life, I could not even cross the street to her without a complicated alignment of permitting circumstances. The truth was – and in my sensory deprivation I was unable to ignore it – I didn't have much to offer Elizabeth. Or for that matter, Philipa (if that were to happen) or Zandy (if she were to ever look at me).

I guessed that one day the restrictions I imposed on myself would end. But first, it seemed that my range of possible activities would have to iris down to zero before I could turn myself around. Then, when I was finally static and immobile, I could weigh and measure every exterior force and, slowly and incrementally, once again allow the outside in. And that would be my life.

The next morning I decided to touch every corner of every copying machine at Kinko's. Outside the apartment I ran into Brian, who was lumbering toward Philipa's, wearing what I suspect were the same clothes he had on yesterday. He had the greasy look of someone who had been out all night. Plus he held his cell phone in his hand, which told me he was staying closely connected to Philipa's whereabouts. His size touched me, this hulk. And after last evening, with my canny near-seduction of his girlfriend, I felt I was Bugs Bunny and Mercury to his Elmer Fudd and Thor.

I decided to pump Brian to find out how much he knew about my night with Philipa. I trudged out my technique of oblique questioning: I would ask Brian mundane questions and observe his response.

'I'm Daniel. I see you sometimes around the building. You an actor, like Philipa?'

Now if Brian cocked his head and glared at me through squinted eyes, I could gather that he was aware of my escapade with his girlfriend. But he didn't. He said, 'I'm a painter,' and like a person with an unusual name who must immediately spell it out, he added, 'a house painter.' Then he looked at me as if to say, 'Whadya think about that?'

His demeanor was so flat that not only did he not suspect me, but this guy wouldn't have suspected a horned man-goat leaving Philipa's apartment at midnight while zipping up his pants. He didn't seem to have a suspicious bone in him. Then he rattled on about a sports bar and a football game. Staring dumbly into his face to indicate my interest, I realized Brian would not have been a cuckold in the grand literary tradition. In fact, he was more like a mushroom.

I had felt very manly when I first approached Brian, having just had a one-nighter with his girl, but now I felt very sheepish. This harmless fungus was innocent and charmless, but mostly he was vulnerable, and I wondered if I was just too smooth to be spreading my panache around his world. 'Hey, well, best of luck,' I said and gave him a wave, not knowing if my comment was responsive to what he had been talking about. Then he said, 'See ya, Slick.' And I thought, Slick? Maybe he is on to me after all.

My Kinko's task was still before me, so I turned west and headed toward Seventh Street, drawing on all my navigational skills. Moving effortlessly from one scooped-out driveway to the next, I had achieved Sixth Street in a matter of minutes when I confronted an obstacle of unimaginable proportions. At my final matched set of scooped-out driveways, which would have served as my gateway to Kinko's, someone, some lad, some fellow, had, in a careless parking free-for-all, irresponsibly parked his '99 Land Cruiser or some such gigantic turd so that it edged several feet into my last driveway. This was as effective an obstacle for me as an eight-foot concrete wall. What good are the beautiful planes that connect driveway to driveway if a chrome-plated two-hundred-pound fender intersects their symmetry? Yeah, the driver of this tank is a crosswalk guy, so he doesn't care. I stood there knowing that the copiers at Kinko's needed to be touched and soon, too, or else panic, so I decided to proceed in spite of the offending car.

I stood on the sidewalk facing the street with Kinko's directly opposite me. The Land Cruiser was on my right, so I hung to the left side of the driveway. There was no way to justify the presence of that bumper. No, if I crossed a driveway while a foreign object jutted into it, I would be committing a violation of logic. But, simultaneously driven forward and backward, I angled the Land Cruiser out of my peripheral vision and made it to the curb. Alas. My foot stepped toward the street, but I couldn't quite put it down. Was that a pain I felt in my left arm? My hands became cold and moist, and my heart squeezed like a fist. I just couldn't dismiss the presence of that fender. My toe touched the asphalt for support, which was an unfortunate maneuver because I was now standing with my left foot fully flat in the driveway and my right foot on point in the street. With my heart rapidly accelerating and my brain aware of impending death, my saliva was drying out so rapidly that I couldn't remove my tongue from the roof of my mouth. But I did not scream out. Why? For propriety. Inside me the fires of hell were churning and stirring; but outwardly I was as still as a Rodin.

I pulled my foot back to safety. But I had leaned

too far out; my toes were at the edge of the driveway and my body was tilting over my gravitational center. In other words, I was about to fall into the street. I windmilled both of my arms in giant circles hoping for some reverse thrust, and there was a moment, eons long, when all 180 pounds of me were balanced on the head of a pin while my arms spun backward at tornado speed. But then an angel must have breathed on me, because I felt an infinitesimal nudge, which caused me to rock back on my heels, and I was able to step back onto the sidewalk. I looked across the street to Kinko's, where it sparkled in the sun like Shangri-la, but I was separated from it by a treacherous abyss. Kinko's would have to wait, but the terror would not leave. I decided to head toward home where I could make a magic square.

Making a magic square would alphabetize my brain. 'Alphabetize' is my slang for 'alpha-beta-ize,' meaning, raise my alphas and lower my betas. Staring into a square that has been divided into 256 smaller squares, all empty, all needing unique numbers, numbers that will produce the identical sum whether they're read vertically or horizontally, focuses the mind. During moments of crisis, I've created magic squares composed of sixteen, forty-nine, even sixty-four boxes, and never once has it failed to level me out. Here's last year's, after two seventy-five-watt bulbs blew out on a Sunday and I had no replacements:

52	61	4	20	29	13	36	45	=260
14	3	62	46	35	51	30	19	=260
53	60	5	12	28	12	37	44	=260
11	6	59	43	38	54	27	22	=260
55	58	7	23	26	10	39	42	=260
9	8	57	41	40	56	25	24	=260
50	63	2	18	31	15	34	47	=260
16	1	64	48	33	49	32	17	=260
=260	=260	=260	=260	=260	=260	=260	=260	

Each column and row adds up to 260. But this is a lousy 8 X 8 square. Making a 16 X 16 square would soothe even the edgiest neurotic. Benjamin Franklin – who as far as I know was not an edgy neurotic – was a magic square enthusiast. I assume he tackled them when he was not preoccupied with boffing a Parisian beauty, a distraction I do not have. His most famous square was a kingsize brainteaser that did not sum correctly at the diagonals, unless the diagonals were bent like boomerangs. Now that's flair, plus he dodged electrocution by kite. Albrecht Dürer played with them too, which is good enough for me.

I pulled my leaden feet to the art supply store and purchased a three-foot-by-three-foot white poster board. If I was going to make a 256-box square, I wanted it to be big enough so I didn't have to write the numbers microscopically. I was, after the Kinko's incident, walking in a self-imposed narrow corridor of behavioral possibilities, meaning there were very few moves I could make or thoughts I could think that weren't verboten. So the purchase didn't go well. I required myself to keep both hands in my pockets. In order to pay, I had to shove all ten fingers deep in my pants and flip cash onto the counter with my hyperactive thumbs. I got a few impatient stares, too, and then a little help was sympathetically offered from a well-dressed businessman who plucked a few singles from the wadded-up bills that peeked out from my pockets and gave them to the clerk. If this makes me sound helpless, I feel you should know that I don't enter this state very often and it is something I could snap out of, it's just that I don't want to.

Once home, I laid the poster board on my kitchen table and, with a Magic Marker and T square, quickly outlined a box. I drew more lines, creating 256 empty spaces. I then sat in front of it as though it were an altar and meditated on its holiness. Fixing my eyes on row 1, column 1, a number appeared in my mind, the number 47,800. I entered it into the square. I focused on another position. Eventually I wrote a number in it: 30,831. As soon as I wrote 30,831, I felt my anxiety lessen. Which makes sense: The intuiting of the second number necessarily implied all the other numbers in the grid, numbers that were not yet known to me but that existed somewhere in my mind. I felt like a lover who knows there is someone out there for him, but it is someone he has not yet met.

I filled in a few other numbers, pausing to let the image of the square hover in my black mental space. Its grids were like a skeleton through which I could see the rest of the uncommitted mathematical universe. Occasionally a number appeared in the imaginary square and I would write it down in the corresponding space of my cardboard version. The making of the square gave me the feeling that I was participating in the world, that the rational universe had given me something that was mine and only mine, because you see, there are more possible magic square solutions than there are nanoseconds since the Big Bang.

The square was not so much created as transcribed. Hours later, when I wrote the final number in the final box and every sum of every column and row totaled 491,384, I noted that my earlier curbside collapse had been ameliorated. I had eased up on my psychic accelerator, and now I wished I had someone to talk to. Philipa maybe, even Brian (anagram for 'brain' – ha!), who I now considered as my closest link to normalcy. After all, when Brian ached over Philipa, he could still climb two flights up and weep, repent, seduce her, or buy her something. But my salvation, the making of the square, was so pointless; there was no person attached to it, no person to shut me out or take me in. This healing was symptomatic only, so I tacked the cardboard to a wall over Granny's chair in the living room in hopes that viewing it would counter my next bout of anxiety the way two aspirin counter a headache.

47,800	51,863	55,448	59,511	1,912	5,975	9,560	13,623	17,208	21,271	24,856	28,919	32,504	36,567	40,152	44,215	491,384
13,862	9,321	6,214	1,673	59,750	55,209	52,102	47,561	44,454	39,913	36,806	32,265	29,158	24,617	21,510	16,969	491,384
47,322	52,341	54,970	59,989	1,434	6,453	9,082	14,101	16,730	21,749	24,378	29,397	32,026	37,045	39,674	44,693	491,384
14,340	8,843	6,692	1,195	60,228	54,731	52,580	47,083	44,932	39,435	37,284	31,787	29,636	24,139	21,988	16,491	491,384
48,039	51,624	55,687	59,272	2,151	5,736	9,799	13,384	17,447	21,032	25,095	28,680	32,743	36,328	40,391	43,976	491,384
13,145	10,038	5,497	2,390	59,033	55,926	51,385	48,278	43,737	40,630	36,089	32,982	28,441	25,334	20,793	17,686	491,384
48,517	51,146	56,165	58,794	2,629	5,258	10,277	12,906	17,925	20,554	25,573	28,202	33,221	35,850	40,869	43,498	491,384
12,667	10,516	5,019	2,868	58,555	56,404	50,907	48,756	43,259	41,108	35,611	33,460	27,963	25,812	20,315	18,164	491,384
48,995	50,668	56,643	58,316	3,107	4,780	10,755	12,428	18,403	20,076	26,051	27,724	33,699	35,372	41,347	43,020	491,384
12,189	10,994	4,541	3,346	58,077	56,882	50,429	49,234	42,781	41,586	35,133	33,938	27,485	26,290	19,837	18,642	491,384
49,473	50,190	57,121	57,838	3,585	4,302	11,233	11,950	18,881	19,598	26,529	27,246	34,177	34,894	41,825	42,542	491,384
11,711	11,472	4,063	3,824	57,599	57,360	49,951	49,712	42,303	42,064	34,655	34,416	27,007	26,768	19,359	19,120	491,384
46,844	52,819	54,492	60,467	956	6,931	8,604	14,579	16,252	22,227	23,900	29,875	31,548	37,523	39,196	45,171	491,384
14,818	8,365	7,170	717	60,706	54,253	53,058	46,605	45,410	38,957	37,762	31,309	30,114	23,661	22,466	16,013	491,384
46,366	53,297	54,014	60,945	478	7,409	8,126	15,057	15,774	22,705	23,422	30,353	31,070	38,001	38,718	45,649	491,384
15,296	7,887	7,648	239	61,184	53,775	53,536	46,127	45,888	38,479	38,240	30,831	30,592	23,183	22,944	15,535	491,384

Clarissa burst through the door clutching a stack of books and folders in front of her as though she were plowing through to the end zone. She wasn't though; she was just keeping her Tuesday appointment with me. She had brought me a few things, probably donations from a charitable organization that likes to help halfwits. A box of pens, which I could use, some cans of soup, and a soccer ball. These offerings only added to my confusion about what Clarissa's relationship to me actually is. A real shrink wouldn't give gifts, and a real social worker wouldn't shrink me. Clarissa does both. It could be, though, that she's not shrinking me at all, that she's just asking me questions out of concern, which would be highly unprofessional.

'How . . . uh . . .' Clarissa stopped mid-sentence to regroup. She laid down her things. 'How have you been?' she finally asked, her standard opener.

I couldn't tell her about the only two things that had happened to me since last Friday. You see, if I told her about my relationship with Elizabeth and of my misadventures with Philipa, I would seem like a two-timer. I didn't want to tell her about Kinko's, because why embarrass myself? But while I was trying to come up with something I could tell her, I had this continuing tangential thought: Clarissa is distracted. This is a woman who could talk nonstop, but she was beginning to halt and stammer. I could only watch and wonder.

'Ohmigod,' she said, 'did you make this?' and she picked up some half-baked pun-intended ceramic object from my so-called coffee table, and I said yes, even though it had a factory stamp on the bottom and she knew I was lying, but I loved to watch her accommodate me. Then she halted, threw the back of her hand to her forehead, murmured several 'uhs,' and got on the subject of her uncle who collected ceramics, and I knew that Clarissa had forgotten that she was supposed to ask me questions and I was supposed to talk. But here's the next thing I noticed. While she spun out this tale of her uncle, something was going on in the street that took her attention. Her head turned, her words slowed and lengthened, and her eyes followed something or someone moving at a walking pace. The whole episode lasted just seconds and ended when she turned to me and said, 'Do you ever think you'd like to make more ceramics?'

Yipes. Is that what she thinks of me? That I'm far gone enough to be put in a straitjacket in front of a potter's wheel where I can sculpt vases with my one free nose? I have some image work to do, because if one person is thinking it then others are, too.

By now the view out the window had become more interesting, because what had so transfixed Clarissa had wandered into my field of vision. I saw on the sidewalk a woman with raven hair, probably in her early forties. She was bent down as she walked, holding the hand of a one-year-old boy who toddled along beside her like a starfish. I had looked out this window for years and knew its every traveler, could cull tourists from locals, could discern guests from relatives, and I had never seen this raven-haired woman nor this one-year-old child. But Clarissa spotted them and was either curious or knew something about them that I didn't know.

Then Clarissa broke the spell. 'What's this?' she asked.

'Oh,' I said. 'It's a magic square.'

Clarissa arched her body back while she studied my proudest 256 boxes.

'Every column and row adds up to four hundred ninety-one thousand, three hundred eighty-four,' I said.

'You made this?'

'Last night. Do you know Albrecht Dürer?' I asked. Clarissa nodded. I crouched down to my bookshelf, crawling along the floor and reading the titles sideways. I retrieved one of my few art books. (Most of my books are about barbed wire. Barbed wire is a collectible where I come from. I admired these books once at Granny's house and she sent them to me after Granddaddy died.) My book on Dürer was a real bargain-basement edition with color plates so out of register they looked like Dürer had painted with sludge. But it did have a reproduction of his etching *Melancholy*, in which he incorporated a magic square. He even worked in the numbers 15 and 14, which is the year the print was made, 1514. I showed the etching to Clarissa and she seemed spellbound; she touched the page, lightly moving her fingers across it as if she were reading Braille. While her hand remained in place she raised her eyes to the wall where I had tacked up my square. She then went to her Filofax and pulled out a Palm Pilot, tapping in the numbers, checking my math. I knew that magic squares were not to be grasped with calculators; it is their mystery and symmetry that thrill. But I didn't say anything, choosing to let her remain in the mathematical world. Satisfied that it all worked out, she stuck the instrument back into its leatherette case and turned to me.

'Is this something you do?' she said.

'Yes.'

'Do you use a formula to make them?' Something about my ability to construct the square piqued Clarissa's interest; perhaps it would be the subject of a term paper she would write on me, perhaps she saw it as a way to finally categorize me as a freak.

'There are formulas,' I said, 'but they rob me of the pleasure.'

I could tell Clarissa was dying to write this down because she glanced at her notepad with longing, but we both knew it would be too clinical to actually make notes in front of me. So I pretended that she didn't look at the notepad and she pretended that she was looking past it. Problem was, there was nothing past it, just wall.

Then Clarissa said, 'Have you ever thought of using this . . . ability, like in a job?'

'I have, but haven't come up with anything yet, Clarissa.' I had rarely, if ever, called Clarissa by name, and as I said it I knew why: It was too intimate and I felt myself squirm.

'If you were using your talents in a job, do you think it might make going to work less stressful?'

'Sure,' I said, not meaning it. And here's why. I know that I have eighteenth-century talents in a twenty-first-century world. The brain is so low-tech. Any boy with a Pentium chip can do what I do. I could, however, be a marvel at the Rite Aid, making change without a register.

'Daniel, do you have any male friends?' she asked.

'Sure,' I said. 'Brian upstairs.'

'It's good for you to have a male friend. What do you two do?'

'Jog. You know, work out.'

This was, of course, a lie, but it was the kind of lie that could become true at any moment, as I potentially could work out or jog if I chose. I'm not sure if Clarissa had ever seen this masculine side of me before, which must have sent a chill through her. Then her focus was torn away from me by an internal alarm that she couldn't ignore. She quickly checked her watch and wrapped things up with a few absentminded and irrelevant homilies that I took to heart, then forgot immediately. She collected her things and went out the door with a worried look, which I could tell was unrelated to our session.

The next morning I woke up to the sound of Philipa's stereo. I can never make out actual songs; I can only hear a thumping bass line that is delivered through my pillows, which seem to act like speakers. I got up but stayed in my pajamas and swept the kitchen floor, when there was a knock on the door. It was Brian. Uh-oh. What does he know? Maybe Philipa broke down last night and confessed to our indiscretion and now he was going to bust me open. I sifted through a dozen bon mots that I could utter just before he punched me, hoping that someone nearby would hear one and deliciously repeat it to my posthumous biographer. But Brian surprised me: 'Wanna go jogging?' 'Sure,' I said. 'Around the block?' he said. 'I can't go off the block,' I added.

'Okle-dokle,' he said. 'You change, I'll be downstairs.'

I was stunned that after my lie to Clarissa about my passion for jogging, a redemption should materialize so suddenly and so soon. The moral imperative to turn this lie into a truth was so strong in me that I said yes even though I have never jogged, don't get jogging, don't want to jog, especially with The Brian. I might jog with a girl. But I saw this as a way to straighten things out in heaven with my therapist/social worker. I went to my bedroom and put on the only clothes I had that could approximate a jogging outfit. Brown leather loafers, khaki pants with a black belt, an old white dress shirt, and a baseball cap. When Brian saw me in this outfit his face turned into a momentary question mark, then he relaxed, deciding not to get into it. 'To the beach and back,' he said. 'Oh no, just around the block . . .,' I said, trying to thwart him. How do I explain my conditions to him? This lug. 'Okay, around the block,' he said and started off.

Brian, in jogging shorts, ventilated T-shirt, and headband, looked like an athlete. I looked like I was going off to my first day of high school. Brian was disappearing into the distance and I dutifully tried to follow, but instead stepped out of my left shoe. I continued to hop in place while I slipped it back on and began my initial, first ever, run around any block since graduation. Brian took it easy on me, though, and I was able to close the distance between us. I wished Elizabeth were finalizing a deal on the sidewalk as we whizzed past so heroically. We went around the block once, pausing only while a family unloaded kiddy transportation from a station wagon. Brian jogged in place; I breathed like a bellows. When we started up again Brian ran across the short end of the block and I followed. But Brian came to the corner and, instead of turning, dashed across the street. I couldn't follow. I stayed on my block and ran parallel to him with the street between us. Brian seemed not to care that he was violating my aside to him, which obviously he had not understood to be binding. Brian seemed to think that this is what guys do; they jog parallel up the street. Then he suddenly dashed across the street again, joining me on my block, as if nothing had happened. The two jogging guys were together again. I sensed that Brian's betrayal of our pact was done with the same thoughtless exuberance of a dolphin leaping out of the water: It was done for fun.

Even though Brian was moderating the pace for me, I still felt a euphoric wave of my favorite feeling: symmetry. Though he was yards ahead of me, we were step for step and stride for stride. My energy was coming from Brian by way of induction. I was swept along in his tailwind. I was an eagle, or at least a pigeon. But then I saw where Brian was going. He was heading straight, straight across the street. I already knew that Brian did not see my request to stay on one block as an edict; he saw it as a whim, a whim that could be un-whimmed in the heat of athletic enterprise. There before me was the curb, coming up on Brian and hence me. This time, though, I felt my pace slowing but oddly not my sense of elation. I saw Brian leap over the curb in a perfect arc. Oh yes, this made sense to me. The arc bridged this mini-hurdle. If I could arc, I could fly over it, too. The curb could be vanquished with one soaring leap. I was ten paces away and I started timing my steps. Six, five, four, three, two, and my right foot lifted off the ground and I sailed over the impossible, the illogical. The opposing curb timed out perfectly. I didn't have to adjust my step in the street before I flew over it, too, and inertia propelled me into the grass, where I collapsed with exhaustion, gasping for air as if I were in a bell jar. Brian turned around, still jogging in place. 'Had it? That's enough for today. Good hustle. Good hustle.'

My legs were shaking uncontrollably and I was thankful that I was wearing ankle-length khaki pants where my limbs could vibrate in private. Even though I walked back the long way, across three sets of scooped-out driveways, I now knew that I could run across the street at the curb. I could jog over them, fly over them. Brian had liber-ated me, had shone a spotlight on the wherewithal

61

that had always been inside me, but needed to be coaxed out by human contact.

The next morning I sprang out of bed and promptly fell over. Overnight my muscles had tightened around my bones like O-rings. I would have screamed in pain but it seemed inadequate. I lifted myself back into bed while my mind scanned the medicine cabinet. Nose drops. Tums. Aspirin . . . yes! I could legitimately take four. Off I went to the bathroom, which gave me the opportunity to take measure of exactly where I was hurting: everything below the beltline, every connective tissue, every lateral muscle. They hurt not only in use, but to the touch. Next to the aspirin was something in a blue jar called Mineral Ice. The bottle was so old it was a collectible. But it said analgesic on it and I had a vague recollection of using it in college. So I swallowed the aspirin and took the Mineral Ice back with me to the bed and began applying the menthol gel to my legs, my thighs, my buttocks. After a few moments it began to tingle, which I assumed was evidence of its pain-relieving properties.

But oily gels don't stay where you apply them. They ooze. They creep like vines and spread themselves to places they're not supposed to go. Like testicles. Mine had somehow come in contact with the stinging concoction, which was now migrating over the eyelid-thin skin of my genitals like flames consuming a field of blue-grass. And there is no washing this stuff off. In fact, the more soap and water are applied, the worse it gets. Soap seemed to act like an agent, enabling it to transpire deeper into every pore. All I could do was lie there and wait for it to peak. And peak it did. Alps. Matterhorn. I would have cursed the Virgin Mary but I knew it was not her fault, so I cursed Brian, whose fault it most directly was. Forty-five minutes later, the throbbing subsided, but there was still the suggestion of an icy breeze wafting around my testicles until way after lunch. Which reminds me that the taste of menthol somehow infected my tuna sandwich, even though I was careful not to handle it without the waxed paper.

That afternoon, Brian knocked on my door and I knelt down in the kitchen and hid. I was just making doubly sure that there would not be a second invite to go racing around the block at blinding jock speed.

By the second day my hard line toward Brian began to soften. I stopped thinking he'd done it to get even with me. After all, he had provided me with an astounding moment of conquest, the recollection of which would momentarily numb my tendons.

Not until the third day did I begin to emerge from my invalid state. My muscles began to return to normal and I assumed they were better for it; yes, I was now in tip-top shape. My mind had sharpened, too, because a plan had begun to form that would impress Elizabeth with my newly found machismo. I would wait until she was showing apartments at the Rose Crest and then jog by at a nice casual speed. This would possibly erase and replace her previously formed image of me as a person to be avoided. The occasion presented itself the next weekend. Saturday was becoming *the* busy realtor day at the Rose Crest, and Elizabeth was in and out hourly with lots of street time spent in front of the potential renters' automobiles for the final sales chat. I was ready to go in my jogging outfit, same brown loafers (with thick socks this time to prevent them from falling off), same khaki pants, and same white shirt, and all had been cleaned and ironed (except for the shoes, though I had thought about it). It was not so much the jogging part that I thought would turn Elizabeth's head but the leap over the curb that I knew would hold the magic. I'm smart enough to know that Elizabeth had no doubt seen dozens of men leap over curbs without her falling in love with the leaper, but I do believe this: When an endeavor is special in a person's life, others discern it intuitively and appreciate it more, like the praise a child receives for a lumpy clay sculpture. And as ordinary as such an event might be, it can be instilled with uncommon power. So I reasoned that my leap, my soaring, arcing flight, would have a hero's impact upon her and would neutralize my earlier flubs.

It was not until 2 P.M. that Elizabeth became engaged in a street conversation that seemed it would last long enough for me to parade my newly cultivated right stuff. There was no time for me to delay, think twice, or balk. I had to do it now. I ran down my apartment steps, took the walkway, cut the corner of the grass, and was heading to the end of the block with effortless but mighty strides. My sudden appearance caused Elizabeth and her clients to look toward me. I liked my pace. Easy, confident. Soon the curb was nigh. I checked traffic out of the corner of my eye. No cars. I began to adjust my step – so many details of the week's earlier triumph were coming back to me! I pictured myself airborne while Elizabeth took it all in. But I was not twenty feet away when a squeezing sensation took hold in my chest. This was the familiar ring of panic. The curb suddenly did not make sense, nor did my impending leap over it. I was rapidly collapsing in on myself, and the curb seemed to have reacquired all of its old daunting properties of impossibility. However, I was still shooting forward like a cannonball when, just this side of the point of no return, I put on the brakes and urked to a cartoon halt, and for a second I was the Road Runner and the curb was the Grand Canyon. I was back where I'd been four days ago, only this time the love of my life, and her clients, were watching. Even as I stood there, barely balanced, drenched in humiliation, leaning over the precipice trying to regain my center of gravity, my mind pumped out one clear thought. It was not the idea of the soaring arc that had liberated me, nor was it the thrill of the pace. It had been the presence of Brian, the person who had so confidently led me, who had made my successful leap so possible. He had allowed me to put one foot in the conventional world, and I was about to place down the other.

But my conventions, it turned out, could not be broken overnight, because they had been forged in my brain like steel, and nothing so simple as longing could dislodge them. By now I was flushed with embarrassment and hoped that Elizabeth had not registered my failure.

Let me tell you about my mailbox. It is one of twelve eroded brassy slots at the front entrance of my building. It is also my Ellis Island, because, as I don't have a phone or a computer, and I disconnected my TV, everything alien that comes to me comes through it first. The Monday after my dismal showing with Elizabeth, I went to the mailbox and retrieved six pieces of mail, took them to my kitchen table, and began sorting them into three piles. Into the Highly Relevant pile went two personal letters, one hand-addressed. In the Relevant pile, I put the mail that wasn't personal even though it was addressed to me – ads, announcements, and so on, because anything with my name on it I consider relevant. Third were the letters addressed to 'resident' and 'occupant.' The Irrelevant pile. I had considered a fourth pile, because to me, 'resident' is quite different from 'occupant,' and I have struggled and succeeded in coming up with a practical usage guide. Yes, I'm a resident and occupant of the Chrysanthemum Apartments, but if I went out on the sidewalk and put a large cardboard box over me and sat on the lawn, it could be said that I was an occupant of the cardboard box but not a resident of it. So 'resident' letters could be sent only to my apartment, but 'occupant' letters could be sent to cardboard boxes, junked cars, and large paint cans that I could stick my feet in. 'Occupant' letters could legitimately be considered Very Highly Irrelevant.

The two letters that arrived that day were not insignificant. The first was from the *Crime Show*, informing me that the taping was completed on my episode and thanking me for my participation. Enclosed was a copy of the waiver I had signed that exempted the producers from all responsibility and made me liable for any lawsuits resulting from my appearance. It was probably not clever of me to sign it, but I wanted to be on TV. Plus, it seemed like it would be the nice thing to do. The letter also informed me that the show would be on several weeks from now and to keep checking my local listings for the exact date and time.

The second letter was an airy breeze of a hand-written note from Granny. I always delay opening her letters in the same spirit as saving the center of the Oreo for last. Granny lives on her pecan plantation in southern Texas (hence, my middle name, Daniel Pecan Cambridge). She is the one family member who understands that my insanity is benign and that my failure to hold a job is not due to laziness. The letter sang with phrases that I swear lifted me like a tonic: 'Life is a thornbush from which roses spring; all the hearts in Texas are wishing for you; I smother you with the kisses that are in this letter.' And then a check for twenty-five hundred dollars fell out of the envelope. The irony is that the one person who gives me money is the one person I wish I could hand the check back to and say no, only joy can pass between you and me. I found it difficult to write back. But I did, stingy with loving words because they don't come out of me easily. I hoped she could read between the lines; I hoped that the presence of the letter in my own hand, the texture of it, the wear and tear it had received on its trip across five states revealed my heart to her. I can't explain why it's easy to tell you and not her how she smooths the way for me, how her letters are the only true things in my life, how touching them connects me to the world. If only Tepperton's Pies had a Most-Loved Granny essay contest, I'd enter and my fervor would translate into an easy win. I could forward her the published piece in Tepperton's in-house journal and she could read it knowing it was an ode to her.

The week had been one of successes and setbacks. There was the triumph of my run with Brian and the failure of my peacocking for Elizabeth. There was my excitement at receiving Granny's letter but then the reminder of my own needy status when the check fell onto the kitchen table. But overall, there was an uptick in my disposition and I thought this might be the week for me to find the elusive Northwest Passage to the Third Street Mall.

The Third Street Mall is in the heart of Santa Monica on a street closed to traffic and has hundreds of useful shops with merchandise at both bargain and inflated prices. But it also has a Pavilions supermarket. I have been suffering along with the limited selection of groceries at the Rite Aid because it's the only place to which I'd mapped out a convenient route. If I could manage to get to the Pavilions, well, it would be like moving from Iraq to Hawaii. From barren canned goods and dried fruit to the garden of Eden. Also, coffee. Jeez, the Coffee Bean, Starbucks. I might not seem like the type who could sit at an outdoor café drinking a latte, but I am. Why? No motion required. It's just sitting. Sitting and sipping. I can't imagine a neurosis that would prevent one from raising one's arm to one's mouth while holding a cup, though given time, I'm sure I could come up with one. I also like the idea of saying 'java.' That is, saying it with an actual intent of getting some and not as a delightful sound to utter around my apartment.

I had tried and failed in this quest for Pavilions before, and I know why: cowardice and lack of will. This time I was determined to be determined, but there would be trials. My initial excursions hadn't allowed for anything less than perfection. The route had to make absolute logical sense: no double backs or figure eights, and the driveways had to be perfectly opposing each other. But if I thought the way an explorer would – yes, there would be rapids, there would be setbacks – perhaps I could eventually find the right path.

Maps, of course, are of no assistance except in

the most general way. Maps show streets, but not obstacles. If only city maps could be made by people like me. They wouldn't show streets at all; they would show the heights of curbs, the whereabouts of driveways and crosswalks, and the locations of Kinko's. What about all those drivers who can't make left turns? Why aren't there maps for them? No, I was forced to discover my route by trial and error. But because I now had a catalogue of opposing driveways and their locations in my head, noted from various other attempts to find various other locations through the years, I was able to put together a possible route before I even started. With a few corrections made spontaneously, on my third attempt I finally established a pathway to the mall, and for three evenings afterward I fell asleep wrapped in the glow of enormous pride.

Having a route to the Third Street Mall meant that I was out in public more, so I had to come up with some new rules to make my forays outside my apartment more tolerable. When I was relaxing at the Coffee Bean having a java, for example, I drew invisible lines from customer to customer connecting plaids with plaids, solids with solids and T-shirts with T-shirts. Once done, it allowed my anxiety meter to flat-line. I got a kick out of the occasional conversation that arose with a 'dude.' One time, while enjoying my coffee, a particular tune was playing somewhere in the background. The melody was so cheerful that everyone in the place became a percussionist one way or another and with varying

70

intensity. For some it was finger-drumming and for others it was foot-tapping. I was inspired to blow on my hot coffee in three-quarter time. But the oddest thing of all was that I knew this song. It was a current pop hit, but how had I come to know it? How had this tune gotten to me, through the mail? Somehow it had reproduced, spread, and landed in my mental rhythm section. While it played, I and everybody else in the Coffee Bean had become as one. I was in the here and now, infected with a popular song that I had never heard, sitting among 'buddies.' And there was, for three long minutes, no difference between me and them.

The chairs and tables of the Coffee Bean spilled onto the mall like an alluvial fan. I grabbed a seat that was practically in the street because I could see at least a full block in either direction. No need, though. Because what went on within the perimeter of the sidewalk café was enough for an afternoon's entertainment. People, I thought. These are people. Their general uniformity was inter-rupted only by their individual variety. My eyes roved around like a security camera. Then I was startled out of my reverie by the sight of the one-year-old who had passed by my window last week. His hand was held tightly by the same raven-haired woman, and he leaned in toward the doorway of a bookstore, straining like a dog on a leash. In answer to a voice from inside, the woman turned toward the door and let the child's hand loose. The boy careened the few steps inside and

I saw him lifted into the air by two arms behind the glass storefront. Everything else in the window was obscured by a reflection from the street. The raven-haired woman was not the mother; this I had gathered. The raven-haired woman I assumed to be a sitter or friend. The child clung to the woman behind the glass, and when I saw that it was Clarissa who emerged from the shop, holding this child, so much of her behavior the previous week suddenly made sense.

On the way home, I mentally constructed another magic square, but one of a different order; this square fell under the heading of 'Life':

Granny	Philipa	Brian
Lorraine	?	Rite Aid
Elizabeth	Zandy	Clarissa

I tried a few things in the empty center square, but nothing stuck; anything I wrote in it seemed to fall out. As I studied the image, this graphic of my life, I realized it added up to nothing.

As I walked home, the day was still sunny and bright. Something bothered me, though: the sight of a mailman coming off my block at two-thirty in the afternoon. The mailman was never in my neighborhood later than ten, and this meant there could be a logjam in my planned events of the day. Earlier, when I trotted down with an elaborately planned haphazard flair to check the mail – jeez, I think I remember whistling – the slot had been empty and I assumed there was no mail to sort, so I foolishly changed my schedule. Oh well, the day had already convoluted itself when I sighted Clarissa on the street, and now I was going to sort mail in the afternoon. Sometimes I just resign myself to disaster.

Most favorite mail: Granny's scented envelopes from Texas (without a check). Least favorite: official-looking translucent-windowed envelope with five-digit box number for a return address. But today, at the godforsaken hour of two-thirty in the afternoon, an envelope arrived that was set dead even between most favorite and least favorite. It was plain white and addressed to Lenny Burns. No return address on the front of the envelope, and I couldn't turn it over until I analyzed all my potential responses to whatever address could be on the back. Which I won't go into.

The name Lenny Burns rattled around in my head like a marble in a tin can. There was no one in my building named Lenny Burns, and the address specifically noted my apartment number. The previous tenant hadn't been anyone named Lenny Burns, it had been a Miss Rogers, an astrologer with a huge pair of knockers. And evidently there was some doubt about whether she earned her living exclusively from astrology. The name Lenny Burns was so familiar that I paused, tapping the letter on the kitchen table like a playing card, while I tried to come up with a matching face. Nothing popped. Finally, I flipped over the envelope and saw the return address, and I wonder if what I saw will send a shiver of horror through you like it did me.

Tepperton's Pies. *Like Mom never made.*

Oops. I suddenly remembered that Lenny Burns was the pseudonym I had used on my second essay in the Most Average American contest, written almost automatically while I ogled Zandy. While I didn't imagine that the contents of the envelope held good news, I also didn't think that it held actual bad news, either. The letter informed me that not only was Lenny Burns one of five finalists in the Most Average American contest, but so was Daniel Pecan Cambridge. And both of them are me.

So the real me and a false me were competing with each other to win what? Five thousand dollars, that's what. And the competition would involve

74

the finalists reading their essays aloud at a ceremony at Freedom College in Anaheim, California. This meant that my two distinct and separate identities were to show up at the same place and time. This is like asking Superman and Clark Kent to appear at Perry White's birthday lunch. The other competitors, the letter informed me, were Kevin Chen, who was, evidently, Asian American, and hence, not average; Danny Pepelow, redhead-sounding; and Sue Dowd, whom I could not form a picture of. I wondered what the legal consequences of my deception would be; I wondered if I would have to blurt out in a packed courtroom that I had been swooning in a lovesick haze over Zandy the pharmacist and therefore this was a *crime passionel*. I calmed down after telling myself that any action taken against me would probably be civil and not criminal, and if they did levy a suit against me, it would be very easy to choke on a Tepperton pie, cough up a mouse, and start negotiating.

The next day, I was nervous about the inevitable arrival of the second pie letter, the one that would be addressed to the real me. This led me to an alternative fixation. I should capitalize it because Alternative Fixation is a technique I use to trick myself out of anxiety. It works by changing the subject. I simply focus on something that produces even greater anxiety. In this case, I chose to plan a face-to-face encounter with Elizabeth the Realtor. I had on one occasion written her a 'get to know me' letter that I never sent because no matter how much I approached it, how I rewrote it, I always sounded like a stalker. 'I have observed you from my window . . .' 'Your license plate, REALTR, amused me. . . .' It all sounded too observant and creepy. Which made me ask myself whether I actually was too observant and creepy, but the answer came up no, because I know my own heart.

I had to admit that my previous plans to impress her had backfired like a motorcycle. It was time to do the manly thing: to meet her without deception, without forethought. I decided to present myself as an interested renter, one who is looking to move up to a two-bedroom to make room for an office, in which I would be working with the renowned writer Sue Dowd on a biography of Mao. This seemed to be the honest thing to do.

I called the number on the rental sign, expecting to get, and prepared to deftly handle, the instructions that would take me through the telephonic maze that would finally connect me to her voice mail. But a miracle happened. She answered. *Crackle pop*, she was on a cell phone in her car. I explained who I was, Daniel Cambridge (a swell-sounding name when I leave out the Pecan), that I live near the Rose Crest, and that I was looking to move up. I left out the part about the Mao bio because, jeez, she's not an idiot.

She told me she was between appointments, had twenty minutes free, and could meet me there in ten. I hardly had time to bathe. Well, okay, I said.

I could postpone my conference call, I said. I hung up and cranked on my shower with stunning accuracy. Perfect temperature with one swing of the wrist. I stepped in, knowing I was on the clock, and yet I still experienced one recurring sensation intractably linked to my morning shower. The flowing, ropey hot water sent me back in time to home, to Texas, to the early hours of the morning. To save money, my mother had always turned off the heat at night, which made our house into an ice hotel. Every wintry morning, as a frosted-over adolescent, I made the chilly jaunt from bedroom to spare bathroom. Stepping into the steamy shower was the equivalent of being cuddled in a warm towel by a loving aunt, and now I'm sometimes rendered immobile by an eerie nostalgia in the first few moments of even a quick rinse. This sensation slowed me down like an atom at absolute zero, even though Elizabeth was at this very moment probably running yellow lights to fit me in.

I was toweling off at the window when Elizabeth the Realtor pulled up in front of the Rose Crest. She remained in the car for several minutes talking to herself. I realized she was probably using the hands-free car phone, at least I hoped she was, as one nut in the family would be enough. I threw on soem clothes and scampered down the stairs, skipping across the street at the driveways. I was overcome with an impression of myself as an English schoolboy. I might as well have been wearing a beanie and short pants. As Elizabeth got out of her car, I appeared from behind her and greeted her with a 'Hello y'all, I'm Deniel Cambridge.' I had not intended the slight country twang that affected my speech. And I do not know, if I perceived myself as an English schoolboy, why my greeting came out as though it were spoken by the cook on a wagon train. I suppose I was confused about just who I actually was at that moment. I had now committed myself to a drawl, and I was rapidly trying to uncommit. So over the next few sentences I fell into a brogue, then a kind of high nasal English thing, then migrated through the Bronx, searching until I found my own voice. I finally did, but not before Elizabeth had asked, 'Where are you from?' to which I saved myself with, 'I'm an army brat.'

I followed Elizabeth up one flight of stairs. She reached into her purse, producing a daunting ring of apartment keys that jangled like a tambourine. There was a delay while she flipped and sorted the keys on the ring, and she managed to open the door on the sixth try. There were three odors inside. One was mildew, one was tangerine, both emanating from the same source: a bowl of fruit rotting in the center of the kitchen table. The third aroma was from Elizabeth, a familiar lilac scent that made itself quite known now that she was contained within the four walls of the sealed apartment. This scent thickened and intensified as though it were pumped into the room by a compressor.

Elizabeth swept the pungent tangerines into a paper bag and stuck them in the waste can under the sink, all the while talking up the glories of apartment 214. She wore a tight brown linen skirt that stopped about three inches above her knees, a matching jacket, and a cream silk blouse with a cream silk cravat. She turned on the air conditioner to max, which intensified the moldy smell, causing us both to sneeze. She flipped on the built-in kitchen television to make the place seem lively and swung open the refrigerator to show me its massive cubic feet interior. Price seventeen hundred a month, she said, first and last, plus a security deposit.

'This is a great building,' she said. 'Usually they want references, but I can get you around it.'

'Don't worry, I have references,' I said, wondering who I meant.

This was the first time I'd had a chance to really see Elizabeth. She had always been either too far away or too close up. Now I could frame her like a three-quarter portrait and see all her details. She was tan. Probably not from the sun, I guessed. She wore several gold rings studded with gems; none was on her wedding finger. She had a gold chain around her neck, at the end of which was a pair of rhinestone-encrusted reading glasses. Her eyes were blue. Not her irises, but her lids, which had been faintly daubed with eye shadow. Her skin had a hint of orange; her hair was a metallic gold, which darkened as it neared the roots. She was a collection of human colors that had been lightly tweaked and adjusted. Her efforts in the area of presentation made me admire her more.

Elizabeth was a prize object. She had picked up beauty tricks from everywhere; she had assembled herself from the best cosmetics had to offer. Any man she chose to be with would be envied, and made complete by her. A man who built an empire would certainly need Elizabeth by his side; he would need her and he would deserve her. I knew now that no matter how much I lied to her, the truth would come out about who and what I was, but I just stood there anyway, continuing my dumb charade while she radiated perfection.

She asked if I also wanted to see a three-bedroom down the hall that had just come up. I must have said yes, because the next thing I knew I was in the apartment next door, being shown each closet and bathroom. This place was unfurnished, and Elizabeth's high heels clacked on the bare floor with such snap that it was like being led around by a flamenco dancer. I looked at the apartment with longing, as it was roomy, filled with light, and freshly painted. No tangerine rot here, and I told Elizabeth, who by now was calling me Daniel, that I would check with my co-biographer Sue Dowd to make sure the size of the place wouldn't intimidate her and thus hinder her writing.

After the ritualized locking of both apartments, Elizabeth led the way back down the stairs and onto the street. She sprung her car trunk from forty feet, reached in it, and handed me a brochure. She stood there on the sidewalk just as I had seen her do so many times from my window. Only now it was me to whom she was saying, 'This is a very desirable area,' and 'Each apartment has two parking spaces underground.' I was in on it. I was in on the conversations I had only imagined. Even after these few minutes of talking with her, spending time with her, trying to see her as fallible, Elizabeth lived on in my psyche as unattainable and ideal, and I was still the guy across the street dreaming beyond his means.

'What is your current apartment like?' she asked.

'It's a one-bedroom. But I'm starting to feel cramped,' I said.

'Is it in this area?'

'Yes,' I said.

'Perhaps I should look at it. I can do swaps, deals, all kinds of things,' she said.

I nodded happily, indicating that I appreciated her can-do, full-service attitude. The thought of Elizabeth in my apartment delighted me; it would be a small tryout of our cohabitation. But I wasn't about to take her on my crazy-eights route to a destination only a few linear steps away. She might look at me askance.

'I could come by tomorrow, or next week,' she said.

'Next week is good.'

'What's your phone number?'

'I'm changing it in two days and don't have the new one yet. We could make an appointment now.'

'You want to give me directions?'

I said sure. 'You come down Seventh Street

toward the ocean.' She began to write in a spiral notepad. 'Make a right on Lincoln, left on Fourth, right on Evans, left on Acacia. I'm at 4384.'

Elizabeth looked at me askance. It didn't take her realtor's mind long to compute that my apartment was right across the street. It seemed absurd not to take her over there now, let alone to have given her directions to a location within skipping distance. She didn't call me on it because I guess she'd seen stranger things, and we made arrangements to meet next Friday, right after Clarissa's visit.

Elizabeth drove off while I pretended to be about to step off the curb. My stall involved bending over and acting as if I had found something urgently wrong with the tip of my shoe. Once she rounded the corner, I took my regular paper-clip-shaped route home, checking the mailbox and retrieving what I already knew would be there, the second letter from Tepperton's Pies telling me that Daniel Pecan Cambridge was in competition with Lenny Burns, Sue Dowd (who, if she turned out to be Elizabeth's half sister would be bad luck for me), Danny Pepelow, and Kevin Chen, who was probably a spy.

It was inconceivable that Clarissa hadn't shown for her Friday appointment. I confess that disappointment rang through me, not only because our sessions were the cornerstone of my week but also because I couldn't wait to observe her from my new perspective of secret knowledge. Something else besides disappointment went through me too; it was concern. For Clarissa not to show meant that something was seriously wrong; she didn't even know how to be late. Her earnestness included fulfilling her obligations, and I guessed she would have called if I had had a phone. I used the hour constructively. I imagined Clarissa's life as a jigsaw puzzle. The individual pieces hovered around Clarissa every time I saw her or thought about her, which now included a small male child, a raven-haired woman, her pink Dodge, her ring-less fingers, her stack of books and notepads, her implied rather than overt sexuality. I stood her next to Elizabeth, her opposite. What I saw was Elizabeth as woman and Clarissa as girl. But something was confusing. It was Clarissa who had a child, and Elizabeth who was trolling for a husband. Clarissa, girl-like, had done womanly things, and Elizabeth, woman-like, was doing girly things. It was Clarissa who was being tugged at the ankles by a one-year-old, her schedule dictated by baby-sitters and play dates, and it was Elizabeth who made herself up every day, whose life was governed by the cell and the cordless. In my mind, Elizabeth was all browns and golds; Clarissa was pastels and whites. And although Elizabeth was adult and smart and savvy and Clarissa was scattered and strug-gling and a student, it was Clarissa who had every adult responsibility and Elizabeth who remained the sorority deb.

I put this information on hold. I turned my focus to the Clarissa rebus I had laid out in airspace above the kitchen table. One piece missing: Where was Clarissa's man? Her impregnator. I assumed he was already gone or in the process of being gone, that he was the source or subject of the distressed phone calls. He had been replaced by Raven-Haired Woman, who, I assumed, was a friend filling in for baby-sitters. Raven-Haired Woman was now demystified into Betty or Susie. Clarissa was living advanced juggling and was probably in a mess. Oddly, I now knew more about my shrink than my shrink knew about me, since I had never allowed her to penetrate beyond my habits, which of course is the point of their existence.

I anticipated my next session with Clarissa because I would see what form her apology would take. Or at least the extent of the apology. If she explained too much, she would reveal too much ('my husband is gone and I'm on my own and couldn't find someone to take care of my one-year-old'), and she'd risk violating what I suppose is a shrink tenet. On the other hand, if she under-explained, she might seem callous. She'd found herself in a spot all right and I was going to enjoy watching her wriggle free, because how she handled it would reveal how she felt about me.

Forty minutes later Elizabeth, former woman-of-the-world turned sorority deb, showed up at my place on her tour through the available apartments of Santa Monica. She mistakenly knocked on Philipa's door, which set Tiger barking. I called up the landing to her and her voice, like a melodeon, greeted me with an 'Oh,' and she turned her scrap of paper right-side up causing the 9 to be a 6. She came down the steps at a bent angle, her torso twisted from trying to see the steps from around her breasts.

I tried to appear richer than I was, but it was hard as I didn't have much to work with. Mostly I had put things away that would indicate poverty, like opened bags of Chee-tos with their contents spilling onto the Formica. I did set out a packet of plastic trash liners because I thought they were a luxury item. She came in and stood stock-still in the middle of the living room. As she surveyed the place, wearing a tawny outfit with her knees thrust a bit forward from the cant of her high heels, she gave the impression of a colt rearing up. Nothing much seemed to impress her, though, as she only seemed to notice the details of my apartment as they would appear on a stat sheet: number of bedrooms, or should I say number of bedroom, kitchenette, cable TV, which she flipped on (though it's not really cable, just an ancient outlet to the roof antenna), A/C, which she tested, number of bathrooms (she turned on the tap, I presume to see if rusty water would come out). I loved it when she looked at my bedroom and declared, 'This must be the master.' Calling my dreary bedroom a master was like elevating Gomer Pyle to major general.

She sat in the living room, jotted efficiently on

her clipboard, and asked me how I was feeling about the apartment across the street. 'Had I decided?' I went into a rhapsody about the complications of my decision, about the necessity of contacting my non-existent writing partner. I had been talking for a minute or so when I noticed a rictus forming on Elizabeth's face. She was looking past me at waist level with her mouth dropped open and her writing hand frozen. I turned my head and looked at the TV, and my mouth went open, and if I had been writing, my hand would have frozen, too. There I was on TV, being shuffled along in mock arrest on the *Crime Show*. There was a long moment before I came out with 'My God, that fellow looks like me.' What filled the long moment was my shock, not at the bad luck of the show's air date and time slot, but at how I looked on TV. The blue parka made me look fat, which I'm not. It made me look like a criminal, and I'm not. The show then jumped to the long shot of me talking to the two policemen. Now we could see my apartment in the background, so there was no use denying the obvious. 'Oh right, it is me,' I ventured. 'I made a bundle off this,' and I nodded up and down as if to verify my own lie. Then I turned to Elizabeth and said, 'All I'm saying there is "I'm talking, I'm talking, I'm trying to look like I'm talking."' She looked over at me, then back to the TV, and I knew that she had identified me as someone dangerous.

This moment was like a pivot. Everything in my little universe swung on its axis and reordered itself. Here's why: Elizabeth, whom I had previously seen only on her turf, or through a window, or in my head, was, now that she had crossed the threshold of my apartment, an actual being who would demand closet space. I didn't even have enough closet space for the clothes she was currently wearing. I knew that I could not share a bathroom with eighteen gallons of hair stiffener, and I began to see how clearly she misfit my life. At the same time, when she saw me on TV, her face hid a well-tempered revulsion. In these few elongated seconds, our magnetic poles flopped as she became ordinary and I became notorious.

Elizabeth must have now viewed my apartment as a halfway house, since she asked me if addicts lived in the building. I said no and did a pretty good job of explaining the TV show, though when I began to explain about the murder downstairs she got the hiccups and asked for water. I felt a small surge of pride because the water from the kitchen tap was not murky or even slightly brown. Her cell phone rang and she spoke into it, saying 'yeah' three times and hanging up. Her tone was as if the person on the other end of the line had heard stress in her voice and was trying to suss out her predicament with questions like, 'Are you all right?' 'Are you in danger?' and 'Do you want me to come get you?' She was out the door, and I looked at her from my spot by the window and felt a twinge of the old longing, no doubt brought on by placing myself in the old circumstances.

After seeing the two women side by side, Elizabeth actually before me and Clarissa in my mind, a thought came into my head that jarred me: Would it be possible to scoop up my love for Elizabeth and steam-shovel it over onto Clarissa? This thought disturbed me because it suggested that the personalities of the two women had nothing whatever to do with the knot of love inside me. It implied that, if I chose, I could transfer my adoration onto anyone or thing that tweaked my fancy. But my next thought set me straight. I knew that once love is in place, it does not unstick without enormous upheaval, without horrible images of betrayal flashing uncontrollably through the mind, without visions of a bleak and inconsolable self, a self that is a captive of grief, which lingers viscously in the heart.

But Clarissa was making the decision easy for me. She reflected light; Elizabeth sucked it up. Clarissa was a sunburst; Elizabeth was a moon pie. So now my preoccupation with Elizabeth became a post-occupation as I turned my Cyclops eye onto Clarissa. Yes, I would always love Elizabeth in some way, and one day we would be able to see each other again. But it was too soon right now. Better to let her handle her own pain, with her own friends, in her own way. But Elizabeth was at fault here. She had destroyed whatever was between us by making a profound gaffe: She met me.

Long after the sun had set, my thoughts continued to accumulate, spread, and divide. What were my chances with Clarissa? None. Clearly, none. In nine months of twice-weekly visits, she had not placed on my tongue one sacrament of romantic interest. And not only that, she spoke to me in the tone one uses with a mental patient: 'And how are we today?' meaning, 'How are you and all those nuts living inside you?' At least Clarissa knows I'm benign. But that is not an adjective one wants to throw around about one's spouse: 'This is my husband. He's benign.'

In spite of the gleaming bursts of well-being that were generated by the idea of loving Clarissa instead of Elizabeth, in the deeper hours of the night I began to look at myself, to consider myself and my condition, to measure the life I'd led so far. I did not know what made me this way. I did not know of any other way I could be. I did not know what was inside me or how I could redeem what was hidden there. There must be a key or person or thing, or song or poem or belief, or old saw that could access it, but they all seemed so far away, and after I drifted further and further into self-absorption, I closed the evening with this desolate thought: There are few takers for the quiet heart.

In the middle of the night I woke spooked and perspiring. I clutched the blanket, drawing it up to my mouth as protection against the murderous creature that no doubt was lurking in the room. I lay still in case it did not yet know I was there. I held my breath for silence, then slowly let it out without moving my chest. Eventually this technique caught up with me and I had to occasionally gasp for air. But no one killed me that night, no knife penetrated the blanket, no hand grabbed at my throat. Looking back, I can identify the cause of my panic. It was that my earlier Socratic dialogue with myself about the nature of love had no Socrates to keep me logical. There was just me, seesawing between the poles. There was no one to correct me and consequently no thought necessarily implied the next, in fact, a thought would often contradict its predecessor. I had tried to force clarity on my confused logic, and this disturbed my demanding sense of order.

Two days later I saw a man in a suit and tie standing on the sidewalk in front of the apartment next door. He was rail thin and for a moment I could have been in Sleepy Hollow except this man had a head and no horse. He swayed from left to right, scanning up and down the block for street numbers. He was all angles as he craned sideways and looked up, twisting at the waist to check an address he held in his hand. This one-man menagerie crabbed along the sidewalk, with his neck moving owl-like as he looked far and close.

When he saw the address above the stairs of my building, it seemed he'd found what he was looking for. He collected himself and came up the steps and knocked at my door.

'Daniel Cambridge?' he called out.

I counted to three then opened the door.

'Yes?' I said.

'Gunther Frisk from Tepperton's Pies,' he said.

We sat chair and sofa; this time with the TV off as I didn't want an errant *Crime Show* to leak into my living room. He asked whether I would be available on March 4 to read my essay at Freedom College in the event I won. 'I would check my schedule,' I said, 'but I can always move things around.'

'I have to ask you a few questions. Your age?'

'Twenty-nine.'

'Married?'

'Engaged.'

'Where do you work?'

'I train boxers.'

He chuckled. 'The fighters or the dogs?'

I made a choice. 'The dogs.'

'Ever been in trouble with the law?'

'No.'

I wondered when he was going to ask me a question to which I wasn't going to lie.

'Are you the exclusive author of your essay?'

'Yes.' I marveled at my ability to answer truthfully with the same barefaced sincerity as I'd displayed on my five previous whoppers.

He explained the judging process to me, made me sign a document promising not to sue, gave me a coupon for a frozen pie, and left. I watched from the window as he walked back to his car, got in it, and sat. He picked up a clipboard from the passenger's seat, gave it a befuddled examination, and then again elongated his neck as he looked

91

out the windshield toward my apartment and back to the clipboard. I've only seen comedians do double takes, but here was one occurring in real life. He got out of his car, once again checking the clipboard against the street numbers. He came up my steps, shuffled in front of my apartment, and rapped a couple of times. I opened the door and saw on his face an expression of bewilderment, as though he had stepped into his shoes in the morning and they were size seventeen.

'I'm sorry,' he said, checking his clipboard. 'I . . . I . . . does Lenny Burns live here?'

We just hung there staring at each other. Thank God my eventual response justified the eternity that elapsed before I spoke.

'Dead,' I said. 'Dead!' My voiced raised. 'Dead at twenty-eight!' I cracked out a half sob, drawing on the same intensity of belief I had employed when I wrote the name 'Lenny Burns' on the essay. For dramatic effect, I reeled backward onto the sofa. Could my experience with the *Crime Show*, I thought, have given me the skills of Pacino?

Gunther stood in the doorway. 'Oh, I'm sorry,' he said. 'Mr Burns lived here?'

'He was a cousin; my third cousin removed from my step-mother's side, but we were like *this*. You can't imagine how sudden . . . everybody in the building loved him.' My sincere belief in what I was saying made me choke up.

'He was a finalist, too . . . just like you,' said Gunther.

'Oh my God, the irony!' I cried. 'We entered together. Lenny loved the idea that he might be typical, and once he got that into his head, he wanted to be the *most* typical. He would have loved to have been a finalist. Why couldn't you have come yesterday, before he passed?'

In the hallway Philipa came by and heard me keening inside. She saw the door wide open and the distressed posture of Gunther Frisk.

She called in to us, 'What's the matter?'

'It's Lenny,' said Gunther, trying to be helpful. 'Lenny died.'

Philipa's face was so blank, so unresponsive, that it was possible to interpret her expression as sudden, catastrophic, morbid shock. I rose and pulled her in, holding her face against my shoulder in comfort. Also so she couldn't talk. I said to Gunther, 'Could you excuse us?' He muttered an apology, acknowledging that he might have just blurted out private information that would have been better delivered by a priest. 'I will contact you,' he said as he backpedaled out of my apartment.

It was a shimmering Southern California day, and the light poured into the Rite Aid through its plate glass windows the size of panel trucks. The merchandise inside broke the light like a million prisms. Candy bars, laid out like organ keys, glistened in their foil wrappers. Tiers of detergent boxes bore concentric circles of vibrating color.

The tiny selection of pots and pans reflected elongated sideshow images. Green rubber gloves dangled from metal racks like a Duchamp, and behind it all was Zandy's yellow hair, which moved like a sun, rising and setting over the horizon of ointments and salves.

I had actual purchases to make at the pharmacy and it was just luck that I fell into the correct rotation that allowed Zandy to wait on me. I was buying sixteen Chap Sticks. This was not a compulsion; this was practical. Ten go in a drawer, and I place the other six around the apartment for handy access. I handed her the cash and she might as well have called me by name, as she referenced every prescription drug I ever took.

'Still taking the Inderal?' she asked.

I had tried Inderal for a while to keep my heart from racing; I was off it now. 'Not much,' I said.

'How'd you like Valium?'

'Left me kind of groggy.'

'You stopped your Prozac.'

'Don't need it anymore.'

'Got a thing for Chap Stick, huh?'

She could have been on a data-gathering mission, or she could have been flirting with me. I couldn't tell which. But it was profoundly intimate for her to know what drugs were flowing through my own personal veins. If a waitress were asking me these questions I would definitely consider it a come-on.

Up close Zandy failed in the perfection department, which made me like her more. The button of her nose was askew, as though someone had dialed it to three. Her skin, though, was so dewy and fresh I couldn't quite turn to go. I picked up my sack of Chap Sticks, and she said, 'Don't forget your change,' and then she added a wonderful thing: She said, 'See ya.' I had to stay there a second and take her in before I was able to unstick my gummy feet from the floor.

It was nearing two and I wondered if Clarissa was going to show up this time. There was no reason to think that she wouldn't, as she had slipped a handwritten note under the door earlier in the week with a sincere but formal apology, promising we would resume the following week at our usual time. I assumed that this was the standard apology that one learns in chapter 15 of the therapist's handbook: Don't give out too much personal information. But the idea of the dispassionate shrink slinking up the patient's stairs and secreting a note under the doorjamb probably wouldn't go down well with whatever board would review such things. Still, Clarissa was only a student and allowed to act like one.

Friday at two o'clock – precisely when the second hand fell on neither side of twelve – Clarissa knocked, pushing open the door that I had purposely left ajar. She said, 'I'm so sorry.' Clarissa was an apology champion. 'Are you all right?' I asked, probing for information I already knew but wanted her to tell me. 'Oh yes,' she said, 'I couldn't get a . . .' She was about to say 'babysitter' and then realized it would reveal too much and she changed mid-sentence to 'I got tied up and there was no way to reach you.'

'Would you like something to drink?' I offered.

'Do you have a Red Bull?'

Red Bull is a potent caffeine-infused soft drink that turns grown men into resonating vibraphones. Drinking a Red Bull is more impressive to me than drinking a bottle of Scotch. Several years ago after my first Red Bull – which was also my last – I got in marksman position on the living room floor, opened a pack of playing cards, and repeatedly dealt myself poker hands. I computed that good hands came in bunches; that one full house in a shuffle implies a possibility of more full houses. And lousy hands in a shuffle only create the possibility of more lousy hands. So Red Bull was not allowed in my house, only because this little episode lasted nine hours. Clarissa's request for the caffeine recharge indicated to me that she was going to have to be bucked up if she was going to make it through my session.

'I don't have any Red Bull but I know who might,' I said.

I excused myself to go to Brian and Philipa's amid protestations of 'you don't have to' from Clarissa. I peered into her apartment and saw Brian flaked out on the sofa, his jaw hanging open like a drawbridge. I didn't have the heart to wake him. I came back to see that Clarissa had settled into the easy chair and was staring at the floor. She was wearing a prim pink blouse that made her look so wholesome it was as if Norman Rockwell had painted a pinup. She had a bloom on her cheeks that lied about her real age. Her face had gentle angles, one rosy thing sloping into the next, and it suggested none of the hardness she must have experienced. It seemed as though she were determined to stay innocent, to hang back even though life was dragging her painfully forward. And all my conjecture bore out because she looked up at me and tried to say, 'And how are you?' She choked it out but couldn't continue. She looked down again and I was stymied. I sat. Oh, this was enough to make me love her, because I was right with her, understanding every second and longing to step in. I didn't even need to know the specific that was troubling her, because to me her halting voice easily stood for the general woe that hangs in the air, even on life's happiest days.

Clarissa didn't apologize for her broken voice, which meant that she was, in these few moments, being personal with me. Her apologies were a way of maintaining distance and formality. She turned toward the window and braced herself up a few inches to see the sidewalk. I knew that soon I would maneuver myself into position to see what she was looking at. Everything seemed to be okay and she turned back to me with an empty sigh. 'Sometimes,' she said, 'I feel like I've been to heaven and been brought back to earth. I've seen how things should be and now I'm here seeing how things really are.' Her head glanced around again.

I got up, folded my hands across my chest, and leaned against the wall. I could see the raven-haired woman on the street, hand in hand with the boy – the same boy I had seen her with at the mall – and I wondered why Clarissa, if she had someone to watch her child, would have them tag along on her work rounds. As I listened to Clarissa and watched the plotless drama on the street, I noted a black Mercedes turn the corner and cruise by. I noted it because it was the second time I had seen it in less than a minute and it was significantly under speed. This second time it passed, the raven-haired woman saw it and took a few steps back. The car slowed to a stop, then reversed itself. Clarissa saw me looking out the window and she rose and turned to me, scared. The car was now stopped in the street, carelessly angled. The driver got out of the car and left the door open, approaching the woman and child. He was groomed like a freshly cut lawn. A trim beard framed his face; close-cut gray sideburns fringed his bald head. His suit was well cut and dark and set off by a stark white shirt. I could hear him yelling and cursing. He was wound tight and unwinding rapidly in front of us.

A horrible chain reaction occurred. The man, who looked like an Armani-clad Mussolini, increased his screaming and made his hand into a beak and began poking at the woman like an angry swan. She was knocked unsteady with each jab but defended herself with angry, equal shouts. But the man lost control and pushed her too hard. She lurched back, tripping. But she was holding the hand of the boy and as she fell, he fell with her. With this blow the chain reaction became uncontained, entering my apartment. I felt the shove that drove the boy to the ground and experienced his terror at the noise and violence. I was down the steps running toward the scene, hearing Clarissa screaming and running behind me, hearing Tiger barking from Philipa's window. I took the steps in threes as the legendary slow-motion of panic set in and turned seconds into minutes. I wondered, in these moments while time stretched itself, why I could not step off a curb but stairs did not present a problem. Why could I not rename the curb to stair step and be on my way? Why do I see the light from a lamp as a quantity and not as a degree? Because it was written on the bulb, that's why. I suddenly knew what my enabler was: language. It was my enemy. Language allowed me to package similar entities in different boxes, separate them out, and assign my taboos. I was at the bottom of the stairs when time caught up to itself. A child's scream broke my thoughts; chaotic and angry voices jarred me. I heard my breath gasp and heave as I turned and headed toward the lawn.

The attacker pushed his voice to a rasp and I heard him yelling cunt, cunt, you cunt. I was barreling across the grass when he turned and grabbed the child's arm, trying to pull him up, but I threw myself between them and covered the boy like a tarpaulin. The man tried to pull me off, but I had clenched my fist around a countersunk lawn sprinkler and I was impossible to move. He began to kick my ribs. Fuck you fuck he said.

He tore at my shirt trying to lift me off the boy, whose shrieks had intensified, had penetrated Philipa's apartment, and had roused an angry superman. For the next thing I knew, the bearded man had been lifted off me and thrown against his car. And I saw Brian holding him there, standing between me and him, while Tiger gnarled a few feet away. The man was foaming and spitting and he swore at Clarissa and jerked himself away from Brian, who was twice his size and a hundred times more a man, and who continued to menace him, forcing him back to his car. Before he peeled away, Brian took his foot and kicked the Mercedes door, which I realized later had probably created a three-thousand-dollar dent.

Clarissa swept up her boy, who was wailing like a siren. She held the back of his head against her and he slowly calmed. The scene quieted, and we stood there in silent tableau, but anyone coming upon us would have known that something awful had just happened. Clarissa approached where I lay in a clump on the ground and asked was I all right. I said yes. She pointed to the raven-haired woman and said this is my sister Lorraine, and I said that's Brian. And Brian stood there like Rodin's Balzac. He looked around, 'Everybody okay?' Yeah, we all said. Then Clarissa urged the child forward and said, 'This is Teddy.' Teddy held up his arm, spreading his fingers and showing me a grass-stained hand. My shirt was torn open and Clarissa touched my exposed ribs. 'Ouch,' I said. And I was pleased that I had chosen the perfect word for the occasion.

After making sure that Mussolini was gone and couldn't see our destination, we five soldiers marched up to my apartment. Brian took charge and I asked if he had a Red Bull and yes, he did. Then I wondered if I had made a mistake; I worried that it might be dangerous for Clarissa to have a Red Bull now, when she was most inclined to load a gun and mow down her child's attacker. I decided to put her on crime watch. If ever there was a moment for my Quaalude-laced wheatgrass drink, it was now, but I had long since decided that spiking punch was a bad idea, bordering on the immoral. Anyway, I was nervous about the chemical collision of an upper and a downer, and wondered if the combination could create a small explosion right in the can.

Teddy scrambled around my apartment on hands and knees, occasionally rising on two feet and moving hand over hand along the windowsill. Brian stood like a sentry and was asking questions like 'Who was that guy?' that never quite got answered. But I did know what he was: an angry, unmanageable tyrant, haunted by imagined slights, determiner of everything, father of Teddy, exhusband of Clarissa. This marriage couldn't have lasted long, as she's young, the boy's an infant, and the husband's too violent to have been with her a long time. I assumed that Clarissa would have left when his monstrous streak first appeared and that he had no reason to hide it once he was in possession of her.

Clarissa's sister, who evidently had flown in from somewhere to stand sentry over Teddy until the crisis passed, was the most upset at Mussolini and also was the most lucid, rattling off all his worst qualities to Clarissa and listing all the legal and practical ways to intimidate him. 'Clarissa, I know you can't hate him because he's the father of your child, so I'll hate him for you,' she said.

Clarissa quaked imperceptibly, and I watched her contain herself. She pulled herself inward, doing what she had to do as a mother: think how she could protect Teddy. She looked around the room as she thought, holding each position for an instant before shifting her head or body. As ideas occurred through her, she would respond to them physically. She shook her head; she would express dismay; her lips would tighten. Finally she whispered, 'I can't go home. Where can I go?'

Lorraine said, 'You can stay with me.'

'No, no,' said Clarissa. 'He knows where your hotel is.'

I said, 'You could stay here for the night. All of

you.' They all looked at one another and knew it was a good idea.

A few hours passed. Brian had secreted Clarissa's car behind the building and parked it in Philipa's space; if Mussolini drove by later and saw her car in the street he would bang down every door in the neighborhood trying to find her. Lorraine and Clarissa were going to sleep in my bed with Teddy between them. I would sleep on the sofa. Philipa brought in a sack of fried chicken, a donation. Tiger smelled it and gave me an imbecilic grin of anticipation. I offered him a leg and tried to switch it at the last second with a palmed dog biscuit, but he wasn't fooled, even after I had smeared it with chicken grease. I made the sofa into a bed with a blanket I borrowed from Tiger, which was covered with a wide swath of dog hair.

As night began to fall I started to worry. When Clarissa went to sleep, she would naturally turn out the lights in my bedroom, which would prevent me from turning out the lights in the living room, which meant I would be sleeping under 1125 watts of power. Later in the evening, I noticed she had left a night-light on, which meant I could kick off the fifteen-watt range light. But that was it. I was attempting sleep in the land of the midnight sun. I turned facedown and buried my head in the cushions. After a restless twenty minutes of pretending, I heard a door creak and then footsteps headed my way. Clarissa's hand touched my shoulder and I turned.

'I just wanted to say thank you.'

'Oh,' I said. 'I didn't do anything.'

'Daniel, I was lying in bed thinking about all this and I realized I won't be able to treat you anymore. It's not proper for you to know all this about me. I'll have to ask them to refer you to someone else.'

'Do the same rules apply even if you're only an intern?' I asked hopefully.

'Even more so. I have to show respect for how things are done,' she said. 'It would be serious for me not to report this.'

Clarissa was Mother Teresa to my leprosy. She leaned in toward me. I watched her lips part and close; I heard her breath between the words. In close, her voice changed. Lower, more resonant, like wind across a bottle top. In close, her beauty trebled. Her hair fell forward and scattered the hard light on her face into softer shadows. Her hand rested languidly on the sofa, palm up, almost like it wasn't part of her, and the pale side of her wrist was lost and wan, longing for sun.

'Thank you for letting us stay here. We'll look for somewhere else tomorrow.'

'You can stay here as long as you need to,' I said.

'We might need to stay here tomorrow. I called his sister. She told me he's got to be back in Boston on Saturday. If he goes, we'll be all right.'

Clarissa squeezed my elbow and then stood up.

'Do you want me to turn out the lights?' she asked.

'No,' I said, 'I want to read.' There wasn't a book nearby and I had never told her of my wattage requirements, so she looked around, momentarily puzzled. But this was such a tiny bewilderment at the end of doomsday it hardly mattered. She retreated into the bedroom, leaving the door cracked open.

As midnight closed in on us, the extraneous sounds of televisions and cars, footsteps and distant voices unwove themselves from the night. I closed my eyes. The light no longer bothered me. I thought of the two women in my bed and the protective sandwich they made that held Teddy in place. My body curled and tightened as if being pulled by a drawstring. I gasped for breath. I pictured myself spread over Teddy like a blanket, but I was watching from above, just as Clarissa watched herself from heaven. The kicks intended for Teddy were taken and absorbed by my body. There was something about having intervened at the exact moment of heart-break that evoked a deepening melancholy, and I hiccupped a few sobs. I then saw myself as the boy, hearing and sensing the blows from over-head, and why did I, rolled up on the sofa clutching a pillow, say out loud, 'I'm sorry, I'm sorry'?

I heard a few small *wahs* during the night, a few footsteps pattering around, and I think we all had a fitful sleep. By 5 A.M., however, nothing stirred except my eyeballs, which delighted in having a fresh ceiling to dissect. Silence had finally struck Santa Monica, which put my mind in the opposite of a Zen state. Rather than my head being empty of thought, every crevice was bursting with facts, numbers, revelations, connections, and products. After I had deduced, or more properly, induced how Aquafresh striped toothpaste is coaxed into the tube back at the factory, I created a new magic square:

Granny	Philipa	Brian
Lorraine	?	Rite Aid
Elizabeth	Zandy	Clarissa

I was lost in the vision of the square, this graphic of my current life, when one of its components, Teddy, creaked open my bedroom door and crawled a few feet into the living room, pausing on all fours. The component looked over at me and grinned.

He then made a surprising feint right but went left, then pulled himself up and leaned against the wall, moving his eyes off me only for necessary seconds. He turned and pressed his palms against the wall and then circumnavigated the room until he had gotten to the sofa where I was trying to hard to sleep. He plopped back on his rear end and extended his arms toward me, which I supposed to be some sort of cue for me to pick him up, and I did. I placed him on my chest, where he sat contentedly for about a minute, and I said something that had an intentional abundance of the letter *b* in it, as I thought the letter *b* might be amusing to a one-year-old. I started with actual words – baby, booby, bimbo – then degenerated into nonsense sounds: bobo, boobah, beebow. His expressions ranged from concentration, to displeasure, to happiness, to confusion, to distress, though as far as I could tell, there was absolutely nothing to feel displeasure, happiness, confusion, or distress about. Except for the letter *b*.

I put my hand on his stomach to tickle him and found that my palm extended over his entire rib cage. I picked him up and hoisted him above my head, balancing him in the air on my stiff right arm, which he seemed to relish. I twisted him from side to side and he spread his arms, and for a few moments he was like an airplane on a stick. This simulation of flight seemed to please him inordinately, and his mother, who must have sensed that her boy had gone missing, said from over my shoulder, 'Are you flying, Teddy? Are you flying in the air?'

In the morning, they slipped away like a caravan leaving an oasis, and the return to quiet unnerved me.

The next few days were stagnant. I was distressed to think that my regular visits from Clarissa were over. I wondered how I was going to fill those two hours that had become the binary stars around which my week revolved. I was also concerned for Clarissa, who had not contacted me in several days. I wondered if I had been ostracized from the group because I represented a horrible memory. But on the day and almost the hour of my regular visit, I saw Clarissa crossing the street with Teddy, carrying him under her arm like a gunnysack full of manure. Her other arm toted a cloth bag stuffed with baby supplies that bloomed and poked out of its top.

I opened the door and started to say the *h* in hello, but she cut me off with, 'Could I ask you a favor?' The request held such exasperation that I worried she had used up all the reserve exasperation she might need on some other occasion. 'Could you watch Teddy for a couple of hours?' Without saying anything I came down the stairs and relieved her of the boy. I then understood why she had carried him like a sack of manure. 'He needs changing,' she said. *And how*, I thought. Going in my apartment, Clarissa added, 'I'll change him now and that should hold him.' Clarissa, who was clearly on the clock, rushed the diaper change, pointed to a few toys to waggle in front of him, gave me a bottle of apple juice, wrote down her cell phone number, tried to explain her emergency, said she would be back in two hours, added that Lorraine had gone back to Toronto, kissed Teddy good-bye, hugged me good-bye, and left.

Thus I went from being Clarissa's patient to becoming her son's baby-sitter.

Teddy and I sat on the floor and I poured out the contents of the bag, which included a twelve-letter set of wooden blocks. These blocks were the perfect amusement for us, because while Teddy was fascinated with their shape, weight, and sound as they knocked together, I was fascinated with the vowels and consonants etched in relief on their faces. It was not easy to make words with this selection. Too many *C*'s, *B*'s, *G*'s, *X*'s and *Y*'s, and not enough *A*'s, *E*'s, and *I*'s. So while he struggled to build them up, I struggled to arrange them coherently. Whatever I did, Teddy undid; when he toppled them, I rebuilt them, and when he stacked them haphazardly, I rearranged them logically. Two hours went by and when Clarissa returned, she found us in the middle of the floor, transfixed.

Two days later, I agreed to watch Teddy from four to six and she offered to pay me five dollars an hour, which I refused.

Occasionally I amuse myself by imagining headlines that would trumpet the ordinary events of my day.

'Daniel Pecan Cambridge Buys Best-Quality Pocket Comb.' 'Santa Monica Man Reties Shoe in Mid-Afternoon.' I imagine these headlines are two inches high and I picture citizens standing on street corners reading them with a puzzled expression. But the headline that was now in my mind was prompted by a letter from Tepperton's Pies, which I pinched between my stunned thumb and bewildered fore-finger: 'Insane Man Chosen as Most Average American.' The letter began with 'Congratulations!' and it told me that I had won the Tepperton's Pies essay contest. It went on to describe my duties as the happy winner. I was to walk alongside the runners-up in a small parade down Freedom Lane on the campus of Freedom College. We would then enter Freedom Hall, walk on the stage, and read our essays aloud, after which I would be presented with a check for five thousand dollars.

I was getting a little nervous about the letter's frequent repetition of the word 'Freedom.' It could be an example of a small truth I had uncovered in my scant thirty-five years of life: that the more a word is repeated, the less likely it is that the word applies. 'Bargain,' 'only,' 'fairness,' are just a few, but here the word 'Freedom' began to smell like Teddy's underpants. But what difference did it make? I am not a political person – in college I voted for president of the United States. He promptly lost and I never wanted to jinx my candidate again by voting for him. But whatever was the political underbelly of Freedom College, I was

110

going to make five thousand dollars for reading an essay aloud.

That week I practiced reading my essay by enlisting Philipa to listen to a few dry runs and coach me. Her contribution turned out to be so much more than just a few pointers. Philipa saw it as an opportunity to express to someone, anyone, just how complicated the simplest performance can be. She told anecdotes, got mad, complimented me, sulked, screamed 'Yes!' and generally took it all way too far. Her goal was to impress upon someone, anyone, mainly herself, just how difficult her work was, that a nobody like me needed professional guidance. She almost had me convinced, too, until I realized I was much better when she wasn't in the room.

Friday came and Clarissa dropped off Teddy with a warm thank-you and a bundle of goodies. She gave me a hug that I had trouble interpreting. It could have been, at its highest level, a symbolic act indicating her deepening love for me; at its worst, well, there was no worst, because at its lowest level, it was symbolic of the trust she'd bestowed on me as the temporary guardian of her child. When she left, Teddy burst into tears and I held him up at the window so he could see her. I'm not sure if it was a good idea, because no matter what spin I tried to put on it, he was still looking at his mother leaving. Left alone with Teddy, I then began the game of Distraction and Focus. The object of the game was to Focus Teddy on something he liked and to Distract him from something he didn't. That afternoon I discovered a law that states that for every Focus there is an equal and opposite Distraction and that they parse into units of equal time. Five minutes of Focus meant that somewhere down the line waited five minutes of Distraction.

Within the first hour, I had exhausted my repertoire of funny faces and their accompanying nonsensical sounds. I had held up every unique object in my apartment. I had taken him on my forearm seat and marched him around to every closet, window cord, and cabinet pull. We had stacked and restacked the wretched wooden blocks. In a desperate move, I decided to take him down to the Rite Aid, which I remembered had a small selection of children's toys, and I was hoping that Teddy, the man himself, would indicate exactly which of them would put an end to his frustration.

There was about an hour of daylight left and I toddled him down my street to the first opposing driveways of my regular route. I had a moment of concern about crossing with him in the middle of the street but decided that extra care in looking both ways would ease my mental gnaw. And so Teddy became the first human ever to accompany me on my tack to the Rite Aid. He, of course, had no questions, no quizzical looks, no backsteps indicating he thought I was nuts, and I felt almost as if I were cheating: It seemed to me that if one is crazy, it's unfair to involve someone who doesn't understand the concept. If, as the books say, my habits exist to keep demons at bay, what was the point of exhibiting them in front of someone who was so clearly not a demon? Who, in fact, was so clearly a demon's opposite?

It was dusk, and the interior of the Rite Aid was bathed in its own splendid white light, which democratically saturated every corner of the store. The light was reflected from the polished floors and shocards so evenly that nothing had a shadow. I held Teddy's hand as I led him down the aisles, heading for the toy section. We passed a display of crackers that held him enthralled, and it took some doing to lure him away from those elephantine red boxes spotted with orange circles and blue borders. As I cajoled him with head nods and high-pitched promises of the delights that awaited us just around the aisle, I noticed Zandy looking directly at us from her high perch in Pharmacy. She didn't do anything, including looking away. A customer intervened with a question. She turned toward him, and in the second it took to shift her attention, she turned her face back to me and emitted one silent, happy laugh.

I now had Teddy moored in front of a hanging display of games and toys, and not only did I show him everything, I presented each prospect as though it were a tiara on a velvet pillow. And he, like a potentate reviewing yet another slave girl, rejected everything. He kept looking back and mewing and, unable to point, threw open his palm with five fingers indicating five different directions.

Somehow, and I'm not sure telepathy was not involved, he navigated us back to crackers. This was his choice, and I saw that it was a good one, because what was inside was textural, crushable, and finally, edible.

It was night by the time we left the drugstore. Teddy and I played motorboat and moved into the darkness. The gaily lit Rite Aid receded behind us like a lakeshore restaurant. We walked along the sidewalks and driveways, passing the apartments and parked cars, hearing the occasional helicopter. I held Teddy in one arm and the crackers in another. We came alongside a high hedge bearing waxy green leaves and extending the full length of a corner lot. It was a dewy night but not cold, and there was a silence that walked with us. Teddy held out one arm so that his hand could graze the hedge. He let the leaves brush his palm. He watched and listened, and would sometimes grab and hold a twig to feel it tugged out of his hand as I moved him forward. Soon he established a sequence of feeling, grabbing, and then losing the leaf. I reseated him on my arm so he could lean out farther, and then slowed my walk to accommodate his game and extend the rapture. I came to the end of the block and it was like coming out of a dream.

Clarissa arrived promptly at six to find Teddy and me at the kitchen table in front of two dozen dismembered saltines. The box was torn and bent, and the wrappers were strewn across table and floor. This would have been a mess of the highest order except that nothing wet was involved. We made the transfer and she offered to help me clean up, but I shooed her out, knowing she had better things to do. At the door she said, 'By the way, he's back in Boston and calmed down. He even sent me a support check.' This small comment made me think all night about atonement, about what could be made up for, what could be forgiven, about whether Mussolini's obligatory check meant I should forget about the clobbering I'd received. I decided that the answer would be known only when I saw him again and would be able to witness my own reaction to an offer of contrition.

Speech day at Freedom College was drawing menacingly close and Philipa continued to rehearse me even though I did everything I could to indicate to her that I was sick of the sound of my own voice and weary of her relentless fine-tuning of me. I performed once for Brian – the first outsider to hear me – and he complimented me so profusely that I felt like a three-year-old who had just had his first drawing taped to the refrigerator. Brian then offered to drive me to Anaheim on the day of the award, and I accepted, happy to know I would have a familiar face in the audience. Later I realized I had made no plans to get to the event and Brian was my only real possibility. We would leave at 8:30 A.M., he said. It would take an hour and a half to get to Anaheim. The Freedom Walk begins at eleven, and the speeches start at noon, to be over by one. Brian had gotten all this information off the Internet and printed it out for me, which he proudly cited as a demonstration of his growing computer skills.

The night before my speech, I carefully set my alarm for 7 A.M. I double-checked it by advancing the time twelve hours just to be sure it went off. Then I puzzled for a dozen minutes over whether I had reset the clock correctly, and had to redo the entire operation to confirm an LED light was indicating P.M. and not A.M. I carefully selected my wardrobe, choosing my brown shoes, khaki slacks, a blue sports coat, and a freshly laundered white shirt that I was careful not to remove from its protective glassine bag, lest a hair or dark thread should land on it in the night. I put several inches between my choices and the rest of my clothes for speedy access. I showered in the evening, even though I fully intended to shower again in the morning. This was a precaution in the event something went wrong with the alarm and I had to rush, but it was also part of my need to be flawlessly clean for the reading. Two showers less than eight hours apart would make me sparkle and squeak to the touch. My sports coat, a fourteen-year-old polyester blue blazer, had never known a wrinkle and would stand in stark contrast to my khaki pants. My outfit would be smooth, blue and synthetic above, crinkly, brown and organic below. In a perfect fashion world, I knew above and below should be the same, either all smooth blue and synthetic or all crinkly brown and organic. I

116

marveled that, like soy and talc, these two opposites would hang on the same body.

During these hours, I was making a transition from my imperfect everyday world where the unpredictable waited around every corner, into a single-minded existence where all contingencies are anticipated and prepared for. I laid out my hairbrush, toothpaste, socks, soap, and washcloth. I cleaned the mirror on the medicine chest so that I wouldn't see something on it that I would think was on me. This was important, because I wanted absolutely nothing to intrude upon my single and direct line to the podium, and nothing to distract me during the four-and-one-half hours that there would be between waking and speaking.

Knowing I would probably be too nervous to fall asleep on time, I went to bed at eight-thirty instead of my usual ten-thirty, building in an extra two hours to fidget and calm down. I lay centered in the bed, intending to sleep facing the ceiling all night, without inelegant tossing and turning and scratching and noise-making.

I reached for my universal light switch, which was located just out of reach on my bedside table now that I was in the center of my bed. I had to hinge my body over to snap off the lights. Then, there I was, in perfect symmetry. The white sheets were crisp and freshly laundered. There were no body residues from the night before to contaminate me after my shower. I went over my speech in my head, and once I had done that, I allowed myself a moment for self-congratulations. I was, I said to myself, the Most Average American. Most Average, Most Ordinary. I had become this solely through my own efforts, and had succeeded not only once, but twice, with two different essays. I couldn't wait to tell Granny and asked myself why I hadn't already written her with the great news. Of course it was because I wanted to wait until I had the award in hand before bragging about it. It's the Texas way.

In the morning I was only slightly askew. The top sheet and blanket had barely moved. I must have slept at a rigid, horizontal version of 'ten-hut!' that would have made Patton proud. There was an empty moment before I remembered what today was, but when I did, my voltage cranked up and the ensuing adrenaline rush cleared my sinuses.

The first thing I did was to sit on the edge of the bed and go over my speech. Then I stood and delivered it again, this time adding in a few planned gestures. Satisfied, I stepped out of my pajamas and folded them into a drawer, and put on my robe for the seventy-two-inch walk to the bathroom. I took off the robe and hung it on the back of the door. I turned on the shower and waited the fifteen seconds for it to adjust. Stepping under the water, I let it engulf me and was overcome with pleasure. When my delirium abated, I soaped and scrubbed my already clean body.

Out of the shower, my every action was as deliberate as a chess move. Toweling off, folding, hanging, everything going smoothly until hair. I had determined not to comb it but to brush it once, then shake it so it would dry into a flopover. I had done this a thousand times, but today it resisted the casual look it had achieved after virtually every other head shake of my life. However, I had mentally prepared myself for this uncertainty. If I was to style my hair with a head shake, I had to accept the outcome of the head shake. And though I could have picked up my brush and teased it into perfection, I didn't.

Brian arrived on the nose at eight-thirty, and it was a good thing, too, since by that time I had been standing motionlessly by the door for twenty-two minutes, mostly as an anti-wrinkle maneuver. He and I were dressed almost identically except he wore a tie. Blue up top, brown down below, the only difference in our clothes being in designer eccentricities. My white shirt had stitching around the collar; his didn't. My coat was polyster, his was wool, though they both had the same sheen.

'No tie?' he asked.

'Should I?' I answered.

'I think so,' he said.

I went to my closet and retrieved my one tie. A tie that was so hideous, so old, so wide, so unmatchable, so thick, so stained, that Brian made me wear his. 'Come on, buddy,' he said, and we started off. 'Got your essay?' he asked. 'Yes, and an extra set from Kinko's, just in case.' I had folded my speech lengthwise and put it in my breast pocket. This caused a tiny corner of the white paper to peek out from my lapel, which I nervously tucked back in every three minutes for the rest of the day.

Brian had idled the car in the driveway, making it easy for me to enter as I didn't have to step over a curb. I hung my coat on a hanger and put it on a hook in the backseat. He made me co-pilot, handing me the directions and saying, 'We'll take the 10 to the 5 to the Disneyland turnoff then left on Orangewood. We'll save some time because then we'll be headed away from Disneyland and out of traffic.' He backed out of the driveway, telling me to put on my seat belt, but I really couldn't. It would have cut across my chest and left a wide imprint across my starched white shirt. We turned the corner onto Seventh and I stiffened my legs and pressed them against the floorboard, raising my rear end into the air. This kept me in a prone position with my shoulders being the only part of me touching the car seat. I wasn't sure whether I did this to prevent wrinkles or to prevent myself from slipping into a coma. The answer came later when my legs fatigued and I slowly lowered myself down to a sitting position and nothing happened: I did not blow up, faint, or die. But I remained intensely aware that my khaki pants were soon going to be streaked with hard creases across my fly front.

We were now on the freeway and I had focused the air conditioning vent on my pants, thinking it might serve as a steamer. Finally I said to Brian, 'would you mind if I lowered my pants a little?' 'Huh?' he said. 'If I could lower my pants a little,

I don't think they'll get so wrinkled.' 'Sure,' he said, leaving me wondering if nothing disturbed Brian, ever.

I unbuckled my belt and lowered my trousers to my thighs. I skooched down in my seat so my pant legs ballooned out to keep them from wrinkling, too. I aimed the air vent at my shirt, which bellowed like a sail, preventing even more wrinkling. Satisfied, I then turned to Brian and said, 'I really appreciate you taking me.'

Considering he was driving, Brian looked at me a dangerously long time, but absolutely nothing registered on his face. Even when he was pummeling Mussolini, his face had never changed from its Mount Rushmore glare.

We did have a few laughs as we wheeled down the Santa Ana Freeway. Small industrial neighborhoods lined the access roads and Brian pointed out a factory sign that innocently read, A SCREW FOR EVERY PURPOSE. He found this hilarious, and because he did, I did. As we neared Disneyland, traffic thickened and Brian said don't worry, because right up here we go the other way. Every other car on the road was an SUV, and Brian's green Lincoln rode so low that we were like the *Merrimac* in a sea of ocean liners.

Brian was right. Everyone was turning west toward Disneyland when we were turning east, which meant we avoided a horrendous wait at the freeway exit. We ended up on a wide-open four-lane street that headed toward a few low hills, while behind us soared the Matterhorn. I consulted the directions and soon we were entering what I would describe as a wealthy parking lot. There were wide lanes for access and every third space was separated from the next by grass-filled islands. Trees lined the rows making it all look like an automotive *allée*. In the distance on a hill, stood – or sat – Freedom College, announced by a gilt sign tastefully engraved in a large plank of oak. The bottom line of the sign read, 'PRIVATELY FUNDED.'

At one end of the parking lot was an open tent with a banner promoting Tepperton's Pies and something about Freedom Day. There were twenty or so people milling around; there were tables where students were signing people in, and also several official-looking ladies and gentlemen in blazers, including my contact with Tepperton, Gunther Frisk. Gunther was decked out in a tartan suit, the plaid just subtle enough to keep him from looking absurd. His body was so incongruous with itself that it looked like he had been made by three separate gods, each with a different blueprint for humanity. 'That must be where we're supposed to go,' said Brian, and he turned off the engine. I laid my shirt over my underwear as flatly as possible, and then gingerly pulled up my pants and closed them over my shirttail. I raised to my prone position, opened the car door, and angled my legs onto the asphalt with as little bend as possible. I took my coat off the hanger and slipped it over my shoulders, tucking my protruding notes back in my coat pocket. I surveyed myself and was deeply pleased that very little wrinkle damage had been done to my fly front. In fact, I looked nearly as crisp as I had when I exited my front door in Santa Monica.

Gunther Frisk spotted us and shot out of the crowd as though he were launched. 'Yoo-hoo . . . here, here!' he shouted, as he flailed and waved. We made our way toward the tent, but the parking lot had an uphill trend that made me worry about sweating into my cotton shirt, so I slowed to a rhino pace, which forced Brian, who was walking at a normal speed, to retard his tempo so I could catch up. After Brian introduced himself as my manager, Gunther directed us into the tent, where we were handed a packet of welcoming materials. We had our pictures snapped and two minutes later were given laminated photo IDs threaded through cords that were to hang from our necks like a referee's whistle. In one corner of the tent stood a clump of misfits, the other winners. Sue Dowd, with a body like the Capitol dome – a small head with a rotunda underneath; Kevin Chen, an Asian with an Afro; and Danny Pepelow, a kind of goon. And me. The only one missing was the recently evaporated Lenny Burns.

We were introduced all around, and honestly, it was clear I was the normal one. But as motley as we were, I suspected there was a unifying thread that ran through us all. It was a by-product of the instinct that made each one of us pick up the Tepperton's entry form and sit home alone in our rooms writing our essays. The quality was decency. But it had not really been earned. It was a trait that nebbishes acquire by default because of our inability to act upon the world with a force greater than a nudge. I stood there that day as a winner but feeling like a loser because of the company I kept. We weren't the elite of anything, we weren't the handsome ones with self-portraits hanging over their fireplaces or the swish moderns who were out speaking slang at a posh hotel bar. We were all lonely hearts who deemed that writing our essays might help us get a little attention. We were the winners of the Tepperton's Pies essay contest, and I, at least for today, was their king.

This sinking feeling did not last. I reminded myself that my entry into the contest had been a lark and that it had really been done to extend my Rite Aid visit by a few extra Zandy-filled minutes, though I guessed that my competitors had taken their efforts seriously. I thought of them slunk over their writing pads with their pencils gripped like javelins and their blue tongues sticking out in brain-squeezing concentration. The spell was also broken by Gunther Frisk's triple hand-clap and cry of 'All right, people.' It was time, he said, to start the Freedom Walk. He tried to gather us into a little regiment, but there were enough docents and officials trailing us to make the group seem a bit ragtag. We trudged up a concrete pathway. I needed to walk slowly enough as to not break a sweat, so I cleverly started at the front of the group, hoping that by the end of the march I wouldn't be too far behind. The sun beat down on me and I worried about a sunburn singeing one cheek, or the heat causing a layer of oily skin that would make my forehead shine under the spotlight like a lard-smeared cookie pan.

The top of the hill held an unholy sight. It turns out that Freedom College is a little village, pristine and fresh, with its classrooms set back on fertile lawns surrounded by low wrought-iron gates. In front of each of these bungalows, hung from natural wood supports, were white signs with the name of each department in calligraphic script, and each compound was set on its own block, with a street in front of it, with sidewalks. And curbs. Curbs I had not counted on. In all my preparations for this day, the problem of curbs never occurred to me. Yes, there was the occasional access driveway for supply trucks, but they were never opposed by another driveway or were in some way askew. And worse, students of both sexes, sporting matching blazers, lined most of the sidewalks to hail our arrival, creating an audience for my terror. Our troop had gathered a small head of steam and was not about to regroup or swerve for my unexplainable impulses. The pathway fed onto a sidewalk and I saw that I was on a direct path to curb confrontation.

False hopes arose in me. Perhaps, I thought, the other contestants too could not cross curbs. But I knew the odds of finding anyone else whose neuroses had jelled into curb fear were slim. Perhaps my behavior would be canceled out by someone else's even more extravagant compulsion. Perhaps we'd find out that Danny Pepelow needed to sit in a trash can and bark. Maybe Sue Dowd couldn't go a full hour without putting a silver Jiffy Pop bag over her head. But no rescue was materializing and the curb was nigh. I could turn back. I did not have to speak at Freedom Hall, I said to myself. I could stop and cower in front of the curb, collapsed in a pool of stinking sweat, weeping and moaning, 'No, no, I can't cross it,' or I could simply move backward while everyone looked at me and my ashen face and my moon-walking feet. These cowardly solutions were complicated by another powerful force, the fear of public humiliation. The students had started to applaud thinly, probably because they had been instructed to. My fear of the curb and my fear of embarrassment clashed, and my extremities turned cold. My hands trembled with the chill. I felt greatly out of balance and widened my stance to keep from reeling. I breathed deeply to calm myself, but instead, my pulse raced into the danger zone.

If I'd allowed my body to do what it wanted to do, it would have fallen on its knees and its head on the ground, its arms stretched out on the sidewalk. Its mind would have roiled and its throat would have cried, and nothing but exhaustion would have made it all stop, and nothing but home could have set the scale back in balance. But instead, I marched on, spurred by intertia and the infinitesimal recollection that I had recently crossed a curb and had not died.

My feet were like anvils, and it seemed as if the curb were nearing me rather than I nearing it. My fear represented the failure of the human system. It is a sad truth of our creation: Something is amiss in our design, there are loose ends of our psychology that are simply not wrapped up. My fears were the dirty secrets of evolution. They were not provided for, and I was forced to construct elaborate temples to house them.

As I neared the curb, my gait slowed. Most of the party had passed me and was happily, thoughtlessly mid-street. Even Brian, who at first had hung back, was now even with me, and as we approached the curb we were stride for stride, our arms swinging in time like a metronome. Just before Brian stepped off the curb, I slipped my index finger into the cuff of his jacket and clipped my thumb against it. I was hanging on to him for my life. I don't think Brian could feel my minuscule clamp on his coat sleeve. As I raised my foot into the air above the road, I relived Brian as leader, how his leap across my curb weeks ago had shot me over it, too, how his he-man engine had somehow revved up mine. My foot landed on the street and it was like diving into icy water. The sound of the clapping students became more and more distant as I submerged, and I kept my fingers secretly clasped to my lifeline.

When the next curb appeared I came up for air and stepped up onto the sidewalk. Muffled sounds began to clear and sharpen. By now, Brian had felt the to-and-fro tug at his sleeve and he turned to me. My blood pressure had soared and had pushed streams of red into my eyeballs and he saw them wide with fear. But Brian seemed to think it was okay that I hung on to him for safety. And I felt safe, too, even though the contact point was only the size of a small fingerprint.

There were four curbs in all and each step down was like the dunking of a Salem witch. I would be submerged into the fires of hell and lifted into the sky for breath. My persecutors were Tepperton's Pies, and my redeemers were my thumb and forefinger pinching a square half inch of wool. When I finally saw Freedom Hall a few yards in front of me, its name now held a double meaning. My pulse lowered to acceptable; my tongue became unstuck from the roof of my mouth. But my God, was I drenched. I attempted to walk so my body would not touch my clothing, trying to center my legs in my trousers so my skin would not contaminate my pants with sweat. I held my arms bowed out so my underarms could aerate and dry, and I could feel that the hair at the nape of my neck was moist and starting to curl.

Finally we were backstage in an air-conditioned office. The chill matched my own body temperature, which had plunged to freezing, and my evaporating perspiration cooled me into the shakes.

My nervousness was increasing and I was afraid that if anyone spooked me I would spring in the air and hiss like a Halloween cat.

Soon we were escorted to the wings, where we stood waiting to be brought onstage. We could hear our introduction through the curtain but the words echoed vacantly and were hardly intelligible. Several students lingered around us and I overheard one of them whisper 'How'd he get away from his gardening job?' and then with a snicker nod his head toward Kevin Chen.

We were told that we would give our speeches in order, 'worst first,' which was quickly changed to 'least votes' first. This meant I would be going last. A stage manager paged the curtain and waved us onstage with a propeller elbow. We entered almost single file, and I realized it was the first moment since I'd left Santa Monica when Brian was not nearby. I looked back. The stage manager had barred him from the wings with a hand gesture.

Out on the stage, the four of us sat on folding chairs while the college dean introduced us one by one. I don't think any of us could make out a word he said. We were behind the speakers and all we could hear was the din of reverberating sound. Occasionally, however, the dean would throw his arm back and gesture toward one of us, at which point we would individually stand and receive enthusiastic applause. From where, I wondered, did this enthusiastic applause generate? Certainly not from the hearts of the audience members, who had no clue who we were or the extent of our accomplishments. I figured it was an artificially instilled fervor, inspired by a version of reform school discipline.

Sue Dowd spoke first, and though I couldn't understand a word she said, I wept anyway. For some reason, her body movements and gestures captivated me. She punctuated sentences with an emphatic fist or a slowly arcing open palm. Her oval body swayed with each sentence like a galleon at sea, and she concluded her speech with her head humbly bowed. There was a hesitation before the applause began, indicating that the audience was either so moved they couldn't quite compose themselves, or didn't realize her speech was over.

Danny Pepelow was next and inordinately dull. When I think of the trouble I went to to dress nicely, I wondered who'd suggested to Danny that a lumberjack shirt, jeans, and leather jacket would be fine. I was able to catch a few words of his essay because he spoke so slowly that the sound waves couldn't overlap themselves. I wondered how he could have possibly gotten more votes than Sue Dowd. At least she gesticulated. Danny stood there like a boulder. His voice was so monotone that I welcomed the few seconds of audio feedback that peppered his speech. He sat down to half the applause Sue Dowd had coaxed, but still grinned as if he had spoken like Lincoln at Gettysburg.

The spotlight then swung to me, but the intro was for Kevin Chen. When the operator heard the

Asian name, the light instantly bounced over to Kevin Chen, provoking a laugh from the audience. He walked confidently to the podium, but I still heard a few racially incited snickers from small pockets of the audience. Kevin Chen was supremely intelligent and quite moving, his essay involving an immigrant family success story with a true and abiding love of America. When he sat down, there was nice applause and I think Kevin Chen had shown them something real that must have touched every heart but the coldest. There was also a specific locus of exuberant cheers from the darkened rear of the auditorium that I presumed was family.

That left only me, and the college dean gave an overly winded intro of which I did not hear a single word. Toward the end of it, though, Gunther Frisk appeared and walked over to him and whispered. Then the dean intoned a few sentences more and I did hear a few words that gave me that icy feeling in my toes and fingertips: 'dead,' 'friend,' 'Lenny Burns.' What? I thought. The dean signaled and waved me over. I stood, and Gunther Frisk met me halfway and hugged me with crushing force. 'I hope you don't mind,' he said. 'Don't mind what?' I asked. 'Don't mind saying a few words about Lenny Burns,' he said, handing me Lenny's essay.

I approached the mike, tapped it, and blew into it; I don't know why. 'It's really Lenny who should have won this today,' I said, knowing that Lenny was me. 'Lenny was a high school friend, and we

131

continued our relationship . . .' Oops. Sounded bad, like we were boyfriends. But I could see the first few rows before they were lost in the lights and they were still a stretch of frozen smiley faces. 'Lenny loved the ladies,' I said, countering myself. I felt I was now even. 'And what is America if not the freedom to love indiscriminately?' I had fallen behind. I said a few more words, each sentence contradicting the last, and I wrapped up with, 'I will miss him,' and managed a little tear in my voice on the word 'miss.' I read a few lines from 'his' essay and secretly knew that had the winner – me – not already been decided, my display of grief over the missing Lenny would have softened the judges and won him a prize right then. I finished the speech with a flourish, stealing Sue Dowd's head-bowing bit, which worked terrifically. Lenny Burns received the applause he deserved, and not just because he died so horribly, as I explained to the audience, from knee surgery gone awry.

I fumbled for my speech, which I realized was not only sticking out of my jacket but about to fall onto the floor. I buttoned my coat and noticed my fly had creased up like an accordion, plus my pants were hanging too low. I pulled them up by the belt, then bent over and tugged at my cuffs to stretch the pant legs straight. This eliminated some of the wrinkles and I felt ready to read. I began my speech with an 'ahem,' a superficial throat clear that I thought showed a command of the room. I spoke the first few sentences confidently, though

132

my voice surprised me with its soprano thinness. Then I noticed the rapt looks on the faces in the audience and felt myself become more impassioned. After all, I was scoring. I invested myself more and more in every word, and this was a mistake, because I began to realize that my speech made absolutely no sense. 'I am average because the cry of individuality flows confidently through my blood'? I am average because I am unique? Well then, I thought, who's not average, every average person? My tricky little phrases, meant to sound compelling, actually had no meaning. All my life an inner semanticist had tried to sniff out and purge my brain of these twisted constructions, yet here I was, center stage with one dangling off my lips like an uneaten noodle. The confusion of words and meanings swirled around my head in a vortex. So I bent down again and pulled at my cuffs. While I was inverted, I was able to think more clearly. I remembered that my speech was not meant to be a tract but more of a poem. More Romantic. And as a Romantic, I had much more linguistic leeway than, say, a mathematician at a blackboard. Still upside down, I reminded myself I was in front of an audience who wanted to be enthralled, not lectured. I decided to reach deep down, to the well-spring of my charisma, which had been too long undisturbed, and dip my fingers in it and flick it liturgically over the audience.

I unfolded from my jackknife bend. My voice deepened and my testicles lowered. I spoke with the voice of a Roman senator: 'I am average,' I said, 'because the cry of individuality flows through my blood as quietly as an old river . . . like the still power of an apple pie sitting in an open window to cool.' I folded my papers and sat down. There was a nice wave of applause that was hard to gauge, as I'd never received applause ever in my life. Gunther Frisk clapped with speedy little pops and leaned into the mike, 'Let's hope he means a Tepperton's Apple Pie!' The applause continued over his interjection and I had to stand again. He waved me over and made a big show of giving me the check, then waved over all the other contestants and gave them the smaller checks. The auditorium lights came up and a few people approached the stage to ask for autographs, which bewildered me. After about four seconds my time as a rock star was over, and I was calmly ushered outside to a golf cart that had been secured by Brian and driven back to his car.

On the way home, Brian gave me several compliments that I discounted and denied. This tricked him into reiterating the compliments, and once he was enthusiastic enough, I accepted them. Then he segued into sports talk, mentioning Lakers and Pacers and Angels, teams I was so unfamiliar with that I couldn't connect the team name with the game. But Brian had been so wholeheartedly on my side that I felt obliged to respond with ardent head nods and 'yeahs,' though I might have misplaced a few, judging by Brian's occasional puzzled looks.

Brian took me to my bank and we barely made

it before closing time. I deposited the five-thousand-dollar check, keeping forty dollars in cash, offering Brian five for gas. Not having driven a car in ten years, I didn't know how stratospherically the price of gas had risen. Now I know the amount was way low for what he must have spent, and I would like to make it up to him one day.

I heard about Granny's suicide before it actually happened. She must have had second thoughts or been unable to pull together the paraphernalia, as her death date fell several hours past the day and minute of my reading of her note. This one lay for just a few hours on my kitchen table before I pulled myself up to it with a jam sandwich and cranberry juice. 'Sweetest Daniel,' it began, and I suspected nothing. Her handwriting was always large and gay, filled with oversized loops and exuberant serifs. Only in the last few years had I noticed a shakiness starting to creep in. 'I won't trouble you with the state of my health, except to say I'm in a race to the finish. I can't let my body drag me down like this without fighting back in some way. My heart is sad not to see you again, but on this page, in this ink, is all my love, held in the touch of the pen to the paper . . .' Then, in the next paragraph, 'I can't breathe, Daniel, I'm gasping for air. My lungs are filling up and I'm drowning.' She said, in the next few lines, that it was time to free herself, as well as the ones who care for her, of their burden. Granny had two Mexican senoras who attended to her, and one of them, Estrella, loved her so much she called her 'Mother.' One last line: 'Finally, we do become wise, but then it's too late.' Granny, dead at eighty-eight of self-inflicted vodka, pills, and one transparent plastic bag.

The news of her death left me disturbingly unaffected. At least for a while. I wondered if I were truly crazy not to feel engulfed by the loss and unable to function. But the sorrow was simply delayed and intermittent. It did not come when it should have but appeared in discrete packets over a series of discontinuous days, stretching into months. Once, while tossing Teddy into the air, a packet appeared in the space between us, and vanished once he was back in my grip. Once, I positioned my palm between my eyes and the sun, and I felt this had something to do with Granny, for it was she who stood between me and what would scorch me. It was not that I missed her; she was so far from me by the time it was all over that our communications had become spare. She lived in me dead or alive. Even now, the absence of her letters is the same as getting them, for when I have the vague notion that one is due, I feel the familiar sensation of comfort that I did when I held a physical letter in my hand.

The day after the letter was Easter Sunday. It reminded me that as an adolescent I was primped and combed and then incarcerated in a wool suit that had the texture of burrs. I was then dragged to church, where I had to sit for several hours on

136

a cushionless maple pew in the suffocating Texas heat. These experiences drained me of the concept of Jesus as benevolent. I did, however, proudly wear an enamel pin that signified I had memorized the books of the Bible.

That Granny's death fell so close to this nostalgic day was just bad luck, and that Easter I lay in bed gripped in a vise of reflection. It was after ten, and although my thoughts of the past were viscous and unbudging, the darkness in the room intensified my hearing, allowing me to keep at least one of my senses in the present. Amid a deep concentration on a potato salad of thirty years ago, I heard a car door slam, followed by hurried steps, followed by a quiet but persistent knock on my front door. I threw on pants and a T-shirt and opened the door without asking who it was.

Clarissa stood before me in a shambles, with Teddy clinging to her like a koala bear. I had not seen either of them at all during Easter week.

'Are you up?' she asked.

'I'm up,' I said, and Teddy, holding out his arms, climbed over onto me. Clarissa came in, glancing toward the street. 'He's back?' I said.

'He was here all week and things were tolerable at least. But today he started getting agitated. It's like he's on a timer. He began phoning every five minutes, which got me upset, then he suddenly stopped calling and I knew what was next. I heard a car screech outside my apartment and I knew it was him, so I got Teddy and bumped his head hurrying him into the car seat.' By now her voice was breaking and she soothed Teddy's head with her palm. 'Can I just sit here or stay here for a minute or maybe the night till I figure out what to do?' But she knew she didn't have to ask, just stay. Teddy gripped my two forefingers with his fists and I moved them side to side. 'Do you have anything?' she asked. 'Any baby wipes or diapers or anything?' I had it all.

We followed our previous routine. Clarissa and Teddy slept in my room, and I slept on the sofa under lights so bright I tanned. Around 3 A.M. there was baby noise and I heard Clarissa's hushed footsteps as she lightly bounced Teddy around the bedroom. Her door was cracked open and I said, 'Everything okay?'

She slid a bladed palm in the doorway, opening it by a few more inches. 'You awake?' she asked. 'C'mon in, let's talk,' she said. We passed Teddy off between us several times as we entered the bedroom. I knew what the invitation was about, camping buddies. But she seemed to have something on her mind of a verbal nature. Clarissa accommodated my lighting requirements by closing the door just enough to create a soft half-light in the bedroom. After a while we put Teddy in the center of the bed, and though he still was wide awake, he calmed and made dove sounds. We were lying on either side of him and I put my hand on his grapefruit stomach, rolled him onto his back, and rocked him back and forth.

'What's going on with you these days?' asked Clarissa.

And I told her of Granny's suicide. 'The funeral is the day after tomorrow,' I said. 'But I can't be there.'

'Do you want to be there?' she asked.

'What could I do there? What good would I be?' I answered.

'I think I should leave for a while,' said Clarissa. 'Would you like me to go somewhere with you? We could drive to Texas, you, me, and Teddy.'

'Too late for the funeral,' I said.

'Yes, but you would be there; you would have shown up for her.'

Upon hearing Clarissa's suggestion, my mind did a heroic calculation resulting in an unbalanced equation. On one side of the equals sign were the innumerable obstacles I would face on such a trip. I could list a thousand impossibilities: I cannot get in an elevator. I cannot stay on a hotel floor higher than three. I cannot use a public toilet. What if there were no Rite Aids? What if we passed a roadside mall where one store was open and the others were closed? What if I saw the words 'apple orchard'? What if the trip took us in proximity to the terrifyingly inviting maw of the Grand Canyon? What if we were on a mountain pass with hairpin turns, or if, during the entire trip, I could not find a billboard bearing a palindromic word? What if our suitcases were of unequal sizes? How would I breathe at the higher elevations? Would the thin air kill me dead? How would we locate the exact state lines? And what if, at a gas station in Phoenix, the attendant wore a blue hat?

On the other side of the equation was Teddy. I could imagine Teddy cooing in the back while pounding arrhythmically on his kiddy seat, and I could imagine ideas for his next amusement streaming through my head from Needles to El Paso and displacing every neurotic thought. I could imagine trying to distill his chaos into order and taking on the responsibility of his protection. And there was Clarissa, who would be seated next to me; who, now that I was no longer a patient, could be asked direct questions instead of being the subject of my oblique method of deduction. I still knew very little about her, only that I was in love with her. These two factors pulled down the scale toward the positive. But I settled the matter with a brilliant dose of self-delusion. I manipulated my own stringent mind with a new thought: What if I could convert one present fear into a different and more distant fear? What if I could translate my fear of the Grand Canyon into a fear of Mount Rushmore? What if I could transform my desire to touch the four corners of every copier at Kinko's into an obsession with Big Ben? But my final proposal to myself was this: What if during the entire trip I would not allow myself to speak any word that contained the letter *e*? This is the kind of enormous duty that could supersede and dominate my other self-imposed tasks. I quickly scanned my vocabulary for useful words – a, an, am, was, is, for, against, through – and found enough there to make myself understood. Thus 'let's eat' would become, 'I'm hungry, baby! Chow down!' I couldn't say, 'I love you,' but I could say, 'I'm crazy about you,' which was probably a better choice anyway. I could call Clarissa by name, Teddy would simply become something affectionate like big man, bubby boy, or junior. One minor drawback, I couldn't say my own name.

This idea of condensing my habits into one preoccupying restriction seemed so clever that it filled me up with ethyl and I said to Clarissa, 'Okay, I'll go.' Even though I had not officially started my challenge, my response was my first stab at an *e*-less sentence.

It was decided we would leave in the morning. Clarissa was afraid to return home to pack; her bright pink car didn't have the stealth we needed for even a night run. She would have to buy clothes on the road. She had a credit card that she said was at its bursting point, with a few hundred dollars left on its limit. She had her cell phone but no charger, so we would have to be conservative in its use. We waited until 10 A.M. when I could withdraw my remaining thirty-eight hundred dollars for the trip.

I got in the car and said, 'It's a long trip for us. I want our roads to know not much traffic.'

'Huh?' she said.

'In honor of our trip down south, I'm trying to

talk Navajo,' I said. Clarissa laughed, thank God, and pulled away from the curb.

We knew we would never get to Texas in time for Granny's funeral, but the journey had another grail: I would be able to see Granny's farm one last time before it was sold due to the lack of an interested relative to run it.

April in California is like June anywhere else. It was seventy by 10 A.M., heading up to eighty. Even though our reason for fleeing L.A. was somber, the spontaneity of our trip inspired a certain giddiness in us, and Clarissa laughed as we pulled up to the Gap and she ran in for T-shirts and underwear and socks. Teddy looked at me from his car seat and burbled while manipulating a spoon. I, the passenger/co-pilot/lookout/scout who was incapable of taking the wheel, wondered what I would do if asked to move the car. Grin, I suppose. After the Gap I hit the Rite Aid, and my knowledge of its layout sped me through dental hygiene, hairbrushes, everything feminine that Clarissa might need on the trip.

'I got you razors and things,' I said. This was going to be easy; I had yet to miss the letter *e*.

I got back in the car and checked the glove compartment for maps. There were a few irrelevant ones, but the California map would at least get us to Arizona. Pinpointing my current parking spot on a map of the entire state of California was impossible, so I hoped that Clarissa knew how to get us out of town. She turned over her shoulder and fiddled with Teddy. Then, she didn't even ask where to go, just started driving south.

The traffic stopped and started along Santa Monica Boulevard, but soon we drove up a centrifugal cloverleaf onto the freeway where Clarissa stepped on it and accelerated to blissful speeds. It was as if the car had grown wings, letting us soar over the red lights and curbs and crosswalks. I wondered if the reason I was crazy, the reason that I had no job, that I had no friends, was so that at this particular moment in my life I could leave town on a whim with a woman and her baby, saying good-bye to no one, speeding along with no attachments to earth or heaven. The moment had come and I was ready for it. We rolled down the windows and the air whipped around us; Teddy chortled from behind. In honor of Philipa's dog, Tiger, I stuck my head out the window and let my tongue flap in the breeze while Clarissa changed the lyrics and sang 'California, Here I Went,' and kept time by thumping her palm on the steering wheel.

There were unpredictable and unaccountable slowdowns until we passed some shopping outlets in Palm Springs, where suddenly the road widened and flattened as though it had been put through a wringer. We pulled in for fast food at lunchtime, barely stopping the car. After four hours of driving we had not lost our zing but had quieted into comfortable smiles and inner glows. Clarissa checked her messages once. She listened, disappointment slithered across her face, and she turned off the Nokia. I took the phone and stowed it in the car door, which had a convenient space for miscellaneous storage.

We continued heading south with the sun still high. I stole the occasional glance and could see Clarissa in relief. Each eyelash was clearly defined against the crisp background of desert and sky. She was an array of pastels, her skin with its pink underglow set against white sand and the turquoise blue of her blouse. I assembled from the sight of her, from memories of her, a clear picture of Clarissa's most touching quality: her denial of sadness. Only the most tragic circumstances could take the smile from her face and the bounce from her walk. Even now, as she fled from terror, she looked forward with innocence toward a happiness that waited, perhaps, a few miles ahead.

Contained in the hard shell case of Clarissa's Dodge, I was remarkably and mysteriously free from the stringency of the laws and rules that governed my Santa Monica life. So I decided to engage Clarissa in conversation. Clarissa must have decided the same thing, because before I could speak, she launched into a soliloquy that barely required from me an uh-huh.

'I think Chris saw me as his dolly,' she said. I knew from her icy inflection on the word Chris that she meant her inseminator. 'But there was no way I could see it until we were married,' she went on. 'He's borderline; that's what I figured. A belligerent narcissist. He needs help, but of course why would someone seek help if one of their symptoms is thinking everyone else is wrong? I think I'm a narcissist, too. I've got a lot of symptoms. Four out of six in the *Diagnostic and Statistical Manual.*'

I didn't know what she was talking about. It seemed to me that 'Chris' was simply a violent son of a bitch. But I didn't have to live with him. If I had to justify someone to myself, I, too, would throw a lot of words at him. The more words I could ascribe, the more avenues of understanding I would have. Soon, every intolerable behavior would have a syntactical route to my forgiveness: 'Oh, he's just exhibiting abstract Neo-juncture synapses,' I would say, and then try to find treatments for abstract Neo-juncture synapses.

The difference now between me and Clarissa was that she was yakking and I was thinking. I felt I was in conversation with her; but my end of the dialogue never got spoken. So my brilliant comments, retorts, and summaries stayed put in my cortex, where only I would appreciate their clever spins and innuendos.

The route from California to New Mexico essentially comprises one left turn. The monotony of the road was a welcome comedown from the emotional razzmatazz of our tiny lives in Santa Monica. We had practically crossed Arizona by day's end, and just shy of the border, we checked into the Wampum Motel, a joint with tepee-shaped rooms and the musty scent of sixty years of transients. It fit our budget perfectly because nobody wanted to stay there except the most down and out, or college students looking for a campy thrill. The antique sign bearing the caricature of an Indian was enough to cause an uprising.

I'm not sure why Clarissa put us all in one room. Since I was paying, maybe she was honoring the budget, or perhaps she saw us as the Three Musketeers who must never be torn asunder. She got a room with twin beds and one bathroom. The lights were so dim in the room that I had no wattage problem. All I had to do was leave the bathroom light on, open the door one inch, and the room would be perfect for sleeping.

This arrangement also provided me with one of my life's four or five indelible images: After an excursion to the Wampum diner, we retired early to get a jump on the next day's drive. While Clarissa showered, Teddy slept securely in one of the twins, buffered on two sides by a pillow and a seat cushion. I had gotten in the other bed and turned out the light. I huddled up, trying to warm myself under the diaphanous wisps that the Wampum Motel called sheets. The room was lit only by moonlight, which seeped around every window blind and curtain. I heard the shower shut off. Moments later Clarissa came quietly into the room, leaving the bathroom light on per my request but closing the door behind her. To her, the room was pitch black, but to me, having adjusted to the darkness, the room was a patchwork of shadow and light.

Clarissa, naked underneath, had wrapped herself in a towel and was feeling her way across the room. I was officially asleep but my eyes were unable to move from her. Standing in profile against the linen curtain and silhouetted by the seeping moonlight, she dropped the towel, raised a T-shirt over her head, and slipped it on. Her body was outlined by the silvery light that edged around her and she was more voluptuous than I had imagined. She then crouched down and fumbled through a plastic bag, stood, and pulled on some underwear. I wondered if what I had done was a sin, not against God, but against her. I forgave myself by remembering that I was a man and she was a woman and it was in my nature to watch her, even though her ease with taking off her clothes in front of me could have been founded on the thought that she did not see me as a sexual creature.

As compelling as this event was, I did not infuse it with either the tangible heat of desire or the cool distance of appreciation. For whichever approach I chose, I knew it was bound to be unrequited, and so my dominant feeling for the rest of the night was one of isolation.

The morning was a blur of Teddy's needs. Things clanked and jars were opened and Clarissa turned herself away for breast-feeding. Though we slept well, we were both tired and car-lagged from the travel. Still, we were on the road by 7 A.M. and very soon we were in New Mexico.

★　★　★

New Mexico held me in a nostalgic grip, even though I had never been there. Only after we'd spent six hours crossing it before arriving in El Paso did I realize what was affecting me. It was that southern New Mexico was beginning to look, feel, and taste like Texas. Northern New Mexico was comparatively a rain forest; it looked as if an extremely choosy nutrient were coursing underground. Rocks burst with color. Rainbow striations shot across the walls of mesas, then disappeared into the ground. Dusky green succulents vividly dotted the tan hills, and the occasional saguaro stood in the distance with its hand raised in peace like a planetary alien.

But southern New Mexico was arid, eroded, and flat. As we drove, Clarissa liked to turn off the air-conditioning, roll down the window, and be dust-blown. I was beginning to sunburn on the right side of my face, and we screamed a conversation over the wind that ripped through the car. She told me that her bank account was being depleted fast, that she was worried she would have to quit school, thus ruining her chances of ultimately achieving a higher income. She said she was concerned that she would have to move back to Boston per her ex's demand, and she didn't understand why her ex even cared about whether they were in Boston as he seldom exhibited any interest in Teddy. All this bad news was delivered without self-pity, as if it were just fact, and I felt a strong urge to cushion her fall as her life was collapsing.

But I lacked any ideas to support her except cheer-leading. I suppose I could have been a moral voice, but I was beginning to doubt my status in that department, too.

Our conversation reminded me that I was also in financial trouble. Granny's intuition had saved me many times, but that form of rescue was now over. I wondered if my pretense of having no need of money, to myself and to Granny, was childish. My paltry government check was insufficient to support my grand – compared to some – lifestyle. I knew that without Granny's occasional rain of money, there was going to be, upon my return to Santa Monica, a housing, clothing, and food crisis.

In El Paso we found a Jimmy Crack Corn motel that fit within my new scaled-down notion of budget. I joked, 'Discomfort is our byword.' To her credit Clarissa laughed and agreed. We stayed in separate rooms as we sensed a wretched bathroom situation, and we were right. Barely enough room for the knees.

The motel had made one attempt at landscaping, a ramshackle wooden walkway arcing over a concrete-bottomed pond. However disgusting it was for Clarissa and me to look into its murk, Teddy considered it Lake Geneva; he wanted to swim, frolic, water ski, and sail in its green sludge. We wouldn't let him come in contact with the mossy soup, so dense that it left a green ring around the edge of the concrete, but I did make paper boats that Teddy was allowed to throw stones at and sink.

In the morning, Clarissa's shower woke me and I could time my ablutions to hers thanks to the paper-thin walls. We cleaned our teeth, peed, and washed simultaneously, enabling me to appear outside my door at the same time she appeared outside hers, and by 7 A.M., with Teddy already lulled into a stupor by the motion of the car, we were on the final stretch to Helmut, Texas.

What happened under the pecan tree qualifies as one of those events in life that is as small as an atom but with nuclear implications.

Clarissa and I had checked into a local motel, just a short hop from Granny's, that practically straddled the Llano River. It was set in a gnarly copse of juniper trees whose branches had woven themselves into a canopy that threw a wide net of shade. We were lucky to have found a low-cost paradise that had a number of natural amusements for Teddy, including nut-finding, water-squatting, and leaf-eating, and it was easy to idle away a few hours in the morning while we laboriously digested our manly Texas breakfasts.

Before lunch, Clarissa drove me to Granny's. I had no recollection of how to get there, though a few landmarks – the broadside of a white barn, a derelict gas pump, a cattle grate – did jog my memory. But when we left the highway and drove among the pecan groves whose trees overhung the road to the farm, I experienced an unbroken wave of familiarity. The trees grew in height and density as we neared the farmhouse, which was sheltered by a dozen more trees towering 150 feet in the air, protecting it from the coming summer heat. The house was a single-story hacienda, wrapped around a massive pecan tree that stood in the middle of a courtyard. The exterior walls were bleached adobe and the roofline was studded with wooden vigas. A long porch with mesquite supports, sagging with age, ran the length of the house on three sides, and a horse and goat were tied up near a water trough. The trees overhead were so dense that sunlight only dappled the house even at this moment of high noon. A few rough-hewn benches were situated among the trees. Attached to the house was a ramada woven with climbing plants, at the end of which a tiled Mexican fountain flowed with gurgling water, completing this picture of serenity.

There were three cars parked outside, two were dilapidated agricultural trucks and one a dusty black Mercedes. We pulled up and got out. A man in a tan suit swung open the screen door. He held a slim leather portfolio that indicated he was official. He said hello to us with a relaxed voice and we heard the first southern drawl of the entire trip. We introduced ourselves and when I said I was 'Dan, gradson of Granny,' there was a frozen moment followed by, 'Oh yes, we've been looking for you.'

Clarissa went off to the fountain to show Teddy its delights. I went into the farmhouse with Morton Dean Argus, who turned out to be the lawyer for the estate. He explained he had driven all the way from San Antonio and had stayed here on the farm for the last three days to sort out issues among the few relatives who had arrived in pickup trucks after the news got out. 'Y'all arrive a half hour later and I would-of been gone,' he said.

Everything useful in the house had been sacked. Everything personal remained. Antique family photos still hung on the walls, but the microwave oven had been removed. The stove, a 1930 Magic Chef Range, was too ancient to loot, the marauders having no idea of its value to the right aesthete chef. A cedar chest filled with Indian rugs had been mysteriously overlooked. There were the occasional goodies, including period equestrian tack used as wall decor, as well as a small collection of heavy clay curios of sleeping Mexicans, whose original bright colors had patinated to soft pastels.

Morton Argus told me that Granny had been cremated and interred on the property under a tree of her designation. He told me that a one-page will had been read and that certain items – really merchandise – had been distributed to a few workers and relatives. My sister, Ida, had been there, he said, and I felt a pang of guilt that my sequestered lifestyle hadn't allowed her to contact me more quickly so I could have met her at the house. It was Ida, he said, who coordinated the dispersal of furniture to a small swarm of needy relatives.

Ida was three years younger than me. She'd moved to Dallas, married young, and borne children, and she seemed untouched by the impulses that took me inside myself. 'Did my dad show up?' I said. Morton asked me his name. 'Jack,' I said. No, he hadn't.

Accompanied by Morton, I nosed through the house and came into a room piled with cardboard boxes and empty picture frames. An oval mirror leaned precariously against the floor. Four wooden kitchen chairs were alternately inverted and nested on each other.

'Anything you want in here?' asked Morton.

'I'll look,' I said.

Morton excused himself, saying he had to sort out some papers. I knelt down and browsed through a couple of boxes. At the bottom of one I found a metal container the size of a shoe box. It had a built-in lock but the key was long gone. I thought it would take a screwdriver to bust it open, but I gave it an extra tug and it had enough give to tell me it had only rusted shut. A little prying and the lid popped up. Inside were a bundle of letters, all addressed to Granny, all postmarked in the late '70s. Two of them had return addresses with the hand-printed initials J.C. They were from my father. I picked up the box, knowing that this would be the only thing I would take from the house.

I found Morton in the living room, which, because of the exterior shade and small windows, was exceedingly dark. He sat in an armchair that had been upholstered with a sun-bleached Indian blanket. He had a handful of papers that he shuffled then spread open and rearranged like a bridge hand.

'Has your sister contacted you?' he said.

'Not that I know of.' I loved my rejoinder, grounded as it was in a fabulous paradoxical matrix, and perfectly *e*-less.

'So you don't know?' he said.

'Know what?'

'You and your sister,' he said, 'are splitting approximately six hundred and ninety thousand dollars.'

I stayed in the house for another hour, glimpsing faint memories as I moved from one room to another. These were not memories of incidents, but were much more vague and beyond my reach. They were like ghosts who sweep through rooms, are sensed by the clairvoyant, and then are gone.

Clarissa and Teddy had wandered far away from the house and now had wandered back. She appeared at the screen door with a 'How's it goin'?' that expressed an impatience to leave. I said goodbye to Morton, slid an arm around Teddy, and lifted him into his car seat, which made him scream. I put the metal box in the backseat and we drove back to the motel.

We sat in the dining room and I could tell that the trip was starting to wear on Clarissa. Our blistering escape had not solved her problems back home. Earlier I watched her call her sister as the phone battery gave out, and now she seemed in her own world, one that excluded me. Then she laid her hand across her wrist and jumped. 'I lost my watch!' she said. She checked around her, then left me with Teddy while she searched the room and car. She returned – no watch – and explained that it had been a gift to herself from herself, and I assumed it had a greater history than she was telling me. Perhaps a reward for a personal accomplishment whose value only she could understand. 'What do you think,' she said, 'are we ready to head home?'

'Now?' I said.

'In the morning.'

'I want to go back to Granny's for an hour or so.'

This annoyed her. She wanted to leave before dawn, and she persevered. 'I need to get back,' she said. 'I don't even know what I'm doing here.' This was the first time Clarissa had had a hint of surliness, but she made up for it later that night.

She and I were bunked in the same room. This motel was the kind a traveler would consider a charming, memorable find, as its architecture and decoration perfectly identified a specific year in a specific decade in a specific location that could not be seen anywhere else. Built in the '30s, the bathrooms had porcelain sinks and tubs that weighed a ton. The rooms were long and narrow and the ceilings and walls were lined with long planks of dark pine. Wrought-iron hardware strapped each doorway and artisan-crafted sconces silhouetted tin cutouts of cowboy scenes through translucent leather shades. Clarissa and Teddy took one end of the room and I slept at the distant other on a sofa bed that sunk in the middle with a human imprint. We had amused each other by spreading ourselves on the floor and playing a game with a deck of cards that at one time had been so waterlogged it was three times its normal height. Clarissa and I tried to play gin, though we struggled to remember the rules, but Teddy made it impossible because he kept grabbing the cards and rearranging them. Clarissa began calling him Hoyle and I would say to him, 'What do you think, Billy Bob, can I play that card?' And he would either pick up the card and drool on it or slide it back to one of us, which would make us laugh.

Clarissa and I were now used to seeing each other in our underwear. We both slept in T-shirts and underpants. She turned out the lights and we slipped into our respective beds. She spoke softly to me from across the room. 'What was it like today?'

'Thanks,' I said.

'For what?'

'For asking,' I said.

'Daniel,' she whispered, I think to say, of course she would ask.

We didn't speak for several minutes. I didn't want to tell Clarissa about the inheritance because I wanted to digest it myself first, and I didn't want anything external to affect our little trio. Then there was a rustle of sheets, then footsteps. Clarissa came across the room and knelt beside my bed. She reached her arm across the blanket until she found my shoulder and laid her hand on it. Her fingers crawled under my sleeve and began a small back-and-forth motion. She rested her head on the bed and her hair fell against my arm. I didn't move.

'Oh, Daniel,' she said. 'Oh, Daniel,' she whispered.

I didn't know what to do.

'I love that you love Teddy.' The upper one-eighth of her body caressed the upper one-eighth of my body. She moved her hand from my shoulder and laid her palm against my neck with a slight clutch.

'We should go to the house tomorrow, if that's what you want. I'm sorry about today. I'm just impatient; impatient for nothing.'

She closed her eyes. My arm, with the bed as a fulcrum, was locked open at the elbow and sticking dumbly out into the room. It was the part a painter would have to leave out if he were going to make the scene at all elegant. I evaluated Clarissa's tender contact and I decided that it was possible for me to put my free hand on her shoulder and not have the action considered improper. I bent my elbow and touched her on the back. She didn't recoil, nor did she advance.

I didn't know if Clarissa's gestures toward me were platonic, Aristotelian, Hegelian, or erotic. So I just lay there, connected to her at three points: her hand on my neck, my hand on her back, her hair brushing against my side. I stared at the ceiling and wondered how I could be in love with someone whose name had no anagram.

Later, she dragged her hand sleepily across my chest and went back to her bed, leaving a ghostly impression on me like a hand-print of phosphorus.

Teddy woke later than usual and Clarissa and I slept through our usual 7 A.M. get-up. By nine, though, we had eaten, packed, and loaded the car. We got to the end of the motel driveway and when we stopped, I said, 'I don't want to go back to Granny's.' And then Clarissa argued, 'But you said you did.' Then I came back, 'It's out of our way.' Then Clarissa said, 'I don't mind. I think you should go.' Out of politeness, we had switched sides and argued against ourselves for a while to show that we understood and cared about each other's position. Clarissa turned right and we eventually found ourselves once again driving among the pecan trees.

There were no cars out front and the house was locked up. I knew what I wanted to do, find Granny's grave. Clarissa said, 'I'll leave you,' and ran after Teddy, who had charged immediately toward the river. I stood before the house and listened to the breeze that rustled through the groves. I decided to walk near the river, upstream, to avoid the bustle of Clarissa and Teddy, who were downstream. I started out, but the pink Dodge caught my eye. I returned to it, felt around under the paper sacks filled with dirty laundry, and got the metal box I had chosen as my sole artifact of my life with Granny. I walked through the forest and came upon a wooden bench – a half slice of a tree trunk – that faced the shallow and crystalline river. There was a hand-painted stone with Granny's name and dates on it, and a small recently disturbed patch of dirt. This diminutive marker was under the tallest and most majestic pecan tree on the farm, and I guessed that was why Granny chose the spot. I sat on the bench and looked toward the river, trying to meditate on this house and land, but couldn't. My mind has always been independent of my plans for it. I reached in the metal box and picked up the small cache of letters. I thumbed through them and took out the two from my father. I read the earlier one from 1979, which was about Granny. It was a snide criticism of how she ran her property, followed by some tactlessly delivered advice on how to fix things.

The second one was about me:

January 8, 1980

Dear G.,
I'm so glad you were able to see Ida before the trip. She's our little heartbreaker don't you think? I have a photo of her with a cotton candy we took at the San Antonio Fair. She looks like an angel. She knows exactly who Granny is too. We show her your photo and she says Granny. She's only four and she seems brighter than everyone around her. The song says there is nothing like a dame and there ain't. I didn't know

159

how much I wanted a girl, but when Ida was born, that was it for Daniel.

The letter went on, but I didn't. Sitting graveside, I knew that these few words would be either my death or resurrection. Two months later, on a still California night, I would know which. It was there that I breathed my last breath in the world that I had created.

Clarissa and Teddy came up along the river. She spotted me and yelled 'hey,' then picked up Teddy and came over. 'Guess what?' she said, holding up her arm. 'I found my watch. I love it when lucky things happen.'

Clarissa fired up the Neon and drove us out to the highway, where we settled into the ache and discomfort of the long road home. We didn't speak for a while, though I kept a broad smile on my face meant to hide my clammy shakes. All of us including Teddy were impatient to be home, and our three-motel trip to Texas turned into just two motel stays on the way back because of Clarissa's driving diligence. She kept us on the road deep into the night, and I often worried that we weren't going to find a motel with a vacancy.

I felt inadequate around Clarissa as we drove. I waited for her to speak before I felt allowed to. I tended to agree with everything she said, which made me not a real person. There were times when we drifted into solitary thought with no awareness of the passage of time. Once we started to again sing 'California, Here I Come,' and I bleeped myself with a loud buzzer tone when words with the letter *e* came up. Clarissa turned to me and laughed, 'You know what we are, we're a mobile hootenanny.' I roared at the word 'hootenanny.' Then we fell to silence again. In Albuquerque we had the best tacos of our lives, and I forced Clarissa to stop at the municipal library for ten minutes where I Xeroxed twenty pages from various investment books while she fluffed and dried Teddy.

Endless road engendered endless thought. Local architecture provoked in me nostalgia that I could not possibly have. Night caused distracting roadside images to fade into nothing. In the backseat was a pile of letters that radiated unease. Flashbacks of Clarissa's moonlit body presented themselves as floating pictures. My father's letter had finally been delivered to its ultimate reader. Over the next few hours, I experienced emotions for which there were no names. I felt like a different kind of pioneer, a discoverer of new feelings, of new blends of old sentiments, and I was unable to identify them as they passed through me. I decided to name them like teas, Blue Malva, Orange Pekoe Delight, Gardenia Ochre Assam. Then I worked on new facial expressions to go with my newly named emotions. Forehead raised, upper lip puffed, chin jutted. Eyes crossed, mouth agape, lower teeth showing.

I would sit in the backseat and hold Teddy on my lap when he was squirmy in his car seat. But when he was sacked out, I would sit in the front and mentally play with my $350,000. What I knew about finance had been gained through osmosis, but I estimated that I could, without risk, get about 6 percent on my inheritance. This meant that I could withdraw $41,747 a year for twelve years before the principal was depleted. Forty-one thousand dollars a year was twice what I was living on now, which I wouldn't really have needed had it not been for my next question to Clarissa. It was 9 P.M. and we were tired. 'Can you slow, and pull off?' I said.

'Here?' she said.

The reason she said 'here' was because we were on the darkest, loneliest highway on the darkest moonless evening. 'It's a fabulous night and us folks ought to pop out and look at various stars.' I spoke with an echo of a drawl to make my *e*-less sentence sound more reasonable.

She slowed and stopped. The mechanical hum of the car had become accepted as silence, but when we got out of the car, the further, deeper silence of the desert shocked us both. Holding Teddy, I leaned against the car and pointed out the dipper, then the North Star, then Jupiter. A meteor caught my eye but Clarissa turned too late. Clarissa and I didn't speak, but this quiet was different from the stiltedness in the car. The air was cold and brittle but was punctuated with surprising eddies of heated winds.

It was going to take some acting on my part to keep her from knowing that my mouth was on a

162

three-second delay from my brain while it tried to eliminate the letter *e* from everything I was about to say.

What I wanted to say was, 'There's a three bedroom at the Rose Crest for rent. Would you and Teddy like to share it with me?' but it was shot through with *e*'s. So instead I slouched back onto the fender and said, 'I was shown a big vacant flat across from my pad. I'm thinking of taking it. If you want to, you could stay. I could watch him so you could study.' There was a long pause. 'You could stay in your own big room. I don't mind waking up with junior on nights you just want to conk out.' I couldn't think of anything else to say, though I wanted to keep talking so I would never have to hear her answer.

'How much is it?' she said.

'I would pay all our monthly bills, food, all that. You could finish school.'

'Why would you do that?' she said.

Because I am insane. Because I am lonely. Because I love you. Because I love Teddy. 'It could work for both of us,' I said. 'I'd watch him and you could go to school.'

'Can I let you know?'

'Naturally,' I said.

'We would be sharing, right?' she said.

She meant, sharing and that's all. I nodded yes and we got back in the car.

Twelve hours later she said, 'I think it could work. You're sure you're okay with it?'

'I am.'

The drive from Granny's had been one of escalating greenery, ending in the sight of home. The scrub of southern Texas had given way to cacti, which had given way to the occasional oasis in Arizona, which had given way to the pines and oaks of California, which turned into curbs and streets. When we finally pulled up in front of my apartment, I stuck my foot out of the car, put it on the grass, and said, 'Sleet, greet, meet, fleet street.' Clarissa looked at me like I was crazy.

Over the next few days, every habit of mine returned with a new intensity, as though I owed it a debt.

There were two letters waiting for me when I returned. One was a kindly but brief note from my sister informing me of Granny and our inheritance, the other from a law firm in San Antonio informing me of the same. Ida's letter, though less emotional than a letter from Granny, still had the same embedded goodness, and I wrote her back apologizing for my years of silence, listing a few of my dominant quirks so she could understand me a bit better. The letter was so good that I copied it and sent it to the law firm, too, though I realized later they could use it against me in court and try to keep the money for themselves. But they didn't.

The FOR LEASE sign was still up at the Rose Crest, but I didn't want to make any moves until the cash was in hand, and the money took several weeks – of course – to become mine. I had to prove who I was, which was not easy. I thought my argument to them – that I was me because no one else was me – was convincing, but it was not what they were looking for. I had to prove my lineage. My documents were vague. I had no driver's license and could not find my birth certificate. Ultimately the legal firm came to a decision; they had no one to give the money to but me, and my sister had vouched for me, so enough was enough and they sent me the dough.

I now had an actual reason to call Elizabeth the Realtor. Not having a phone, I got the address of her company and walked there, even though the route proved to be almost impossible. I wondered if my path, when viewed from an airplane, would spell out my name. Just before giving up, I found a crosswalk for the handicapped that had two scooped-out curbs and used it as a gangplank to get to Elizabeth's block. I left a note that said I was interested in the apartment.

She drove by several hours later and I ran down the stairs before she could get to my door. Elizabeth must have developed an extremely sophisticated wealth detector because she suddenly began treating me as a viable customer who was swimming in cash, even though I was sure that nothing in my behavior had changed. Even after I made her drive me across the street, which wasn't more than twenty steps, she maintained a professional front and showed no exasperation. Or maybe she perceived my indifference toward her and was trying to win me back.

Within the hour, I'd leased the three-bedroom and even negotiated the price down fifty dollars a month. I had another eight days on my monthly rent and I told her I would move in at week's end. I watched Teddy several times that week and Clarissa showed no signs of backtracking.

I was now purchasing a newspaper every day and perusing the financial section. I diligently followed bonds, mutual funds, and stocks and noted their movement. Movement was what I hated. I didn't like that one day you could have a dollar and the next you could have eighty cents without having done anything. On the other hand, the idea that you could have a dollar and the next day have a dollar twenty thrilled me no end. I was worried that on the day my dollar was worth eighty cents I would be sad, and on the day it was worth a dollar twenty I would be elated, though I did like the idea of knowing exactly why I was in a certain mood. But I saw another possibility. If I bought bonds and held them to maturity, then the fluctuations in their value wouldn't affect me, and I liked that their dividends trickled in with regularity. This meant that my mood, too, would constantly trickle upward and by maturity, I would be ecstatic.

In interviewing a series of bond brokers, I sought out someone who could satisfy my requirement of extreme dullness. I felt that the happier a broker was, the shadier he was. If he was happy, it meant that he thought about things other than bonds.

Happiness meant he might be frivolous and do things like take vacations. I wanted a Scrooge McDuck who thought about only one thing, decimal points. Since I was a person whose own personality rose and fell based on the input of another person, meetings with these brokers were deadly. The more somber he was, the more somber I would become, and we would often spiral down together into an abyss of tedium.

I interviewed four brokers at several firms in the Santa Monica area. It was the second one who was stupefyingly dull enough and who gave me a siren's call when I met with his rivals. His name was Brandon Brady, and he was so dreary that I'm sure that the rhythmic alliteration in his name made him faintly ill.

What made me finally choose Brandon was not his colorlessness but my perception of the depth of his narrow, hence thorough and numerical, mind. I was sitting with another broker, whose own deadly personality challenged Brandon's. It would have been a tough choice based on flatness alone. But when this broker laid out his plans for me, he started with a proposal to buy a ten-year bond starting next Wednesday.

'There's a problem with buying a ten-year bond next Wednesday,' I said.

'And what is that?'

'If I buy a bond next Wednesday, ten years later it would come due on a Saturday, but I couldn't cash it in until Monday. I would lose two days' interest.'

He checked his computer then looked at me as if I were a wax model of myself: I seemed like a human, but something was wrong.

And that was that. I went back to test broker number one, who made the same gaffe. But it was Brandon, who, after I had proposed buying a bond next Wednesday, got out a calculator and made a clatter as he ran his fingers over it, then frowned deeply. 'Well,' he said, 'they've got us on this one. Why don't we wait a few days and see what other bonds come up?' I knew I had found my man.

Clarissa and Teddy's entry into the new apartment was biblical. It was as though they had been led into the promised land. Throw rugs of sunlight crept across every bedroom floor, and I had placed cheap plants in every empty corner, copying a home decor catalogue I had found in the mailbox. I marched Clarissa around the place and she took a breath of delight in every new room, which gave me pleasure. I had budgeted for just enough furniture to make the place functional, so it looked a little spare, but if my twelve-year plan was to work, the cash would have to flow as though through an hourglass. Clarissa had some furniture that she coerced a friend with a pickup to deliver, and Teddy's colorful possessions were quickly distributed throughout the apartment. Clarissa installed a phone, which I viewed suspiciously at first, then finally forgot about. The place filled out incrementally, a few framed photos appeared, and by the end of the month it looked as though a family lived there. Except.

Except that the space between me and Clarissa remained uncrossable. Sometimes I felt an intense love coming from her toward me, but I couldn't tell if it was because of Teddy. I gave it time, and it was easy to give it time, because Teddy's antics often kept any serious discussion at bay. If my hand rested against Clarissa's, it was only a moment before I had to move it to snag Teddy. When he ambled around the apartment, Clarissa hung over him like a willow. There was no such thing as a solitary moment. I began to allow a phrase in my head that would never have been allowed across the street. The imperfect ideal. As strict as my life across the street had been, it was just as loose at the Rose Crest. Teddy's chaos left me in structural shambles, and I think I could tolerate it because the source of the chaos was unified. He was a person beyond logic; he was the singularity.

It is disappointing when you discover that the person you love loves someone else. I made this discovery twice. The first was one evening when the three of us sat down to our usual meal. These dinners were the fantastic disorder at the end of my rigorously structured days spent with my nose in financial magazines and reports. I had grown to anticipate them and participate in them with a newfound looseness. Clarissa and I chipped in and had food delivered, and there was a lot of freewheeling talk accompanied by the opening of white paper bags containing napkins and picnic utensils and tuna sandwiches and mustard packets. This crinkling noise and snap of the plastic tops of containers of mayonnaise always sparked us into thrilling recaps of the day's most mundane events, and months later I realized that these half hours were sacred.

After Clarissa had set Teddy in a high chair and thrown a few morsels of tuna in front of him, he fisted a glob of it and stuck it in his mouth, then turned to her and grinned. Clarissa's face beamed and broadened, her focus was only on him; there was nothing else, no apartment, no jobs, no school-work, no life other than the joyful force that streamed between them. And there was no me. I sat and waited out the absorption, which flickered when Clarissa reached for more food and finally both alit back on earth.

Clarissa's studies progressed and she engaged herself in them with fervor, and she grasped the language of psychology quickly. The vocabulary and concepts came easily to her and she hinted that she had an affection for the subject matter that the other students didn't. At night she would catch me up on what she had learned during the day, give me shorthand analyses of syndromes and disorders, and then would go over comments she had made in class to get my opinion of them.

Clarissa was always thoughtful toward me and would express her gratitude for my assistance in her life, and I would thank her in return, which always left her puzzled. The impact she and Teddy had had on me was made clear one afternoon when a packet of mail arrived, forwarded from my old address. One of the envelopes was from Mensa. I opened it and read that it had been discovered that, as I had guessed, my scores had been compromised by human error, and would I like to take the test again? My first thought took the form of a shock: Human error at Mensa? What chance then did McDonald's have, and the Rite Aid, and CompUSA? My second thought took the form of a semantic shudder at the phrase 'human error': Is there any other kind? My third thought was No, I didn't want to take the test again, because here I was having a life, even though it was a pastiche of elements of the life of someone else.

One night I got a phone call from Clarissa asking if it was all right for her to be home later than usual. 'Would you be okay? Were you going out?' she asked, 'Can you watch Teddy; is Teddy okay?' Sure, I said.

Teddy and I had an evening of bliss. He was the model child and I was the model adoptive/uncle/friend. We cavorted on the bed, we played trash can basketball, we played 'Where's Teddy?' at professional levels. Finally a cloud came over him and he conked out on my bed and I slid him over and rested next to him. My lighting rules were still in effect and the soft thirty-watt lamp on my chest of drawers was balanced nicely by the solar glow in the living room. My door was ajar and I could see the front window and door as I lay in relative darkness. I used this solemn time for absolutely nothing, as I drained my mind of thought.

Tonto.

That's who I felt like when I heard the footsteps coming along the second-floor walkway. I thought to myself, 'There are two of them, Kemosabe, and they're coming this way.' I heard Clarissa's voice, then a man's. They spoke slowly, each response to the other delivered in the same whispered tone. Her answers were shy; his questions were confident and cool. They passed the window and I saw him looking at her as she looked down, fumbling for her keys. The door opened and he stood outside while she moved in, putting her purse down and turning around to him. He spoke to her, and he stepped into the apartment. Her hand touched the light switch and the hard overheads went out, sending my body into rigor mortis. But I watched. They spoke again and he put his hand on her arm, pulling her toward him. She responded. He moved his hand, sliding it up under her hair. He drew her into him and rested his forehead on hers, and I watched him close his eyes and breathe deeply to absorb her. His lips brushed her cheek and I saw her surrender, her shoulders dropping, her arms hanging without resistance. His hand went to her back and urged her, pressing her against him. Her arm went up to his waist, then around his back, and he moved his lips around to hers and kissed her, her arm tightening, locking on his back, her other arm sliding up to his elbow. Her head fell back and he continued kissing her, standing over her, then he stepped back and looked into her eyes, saying nothing.

It is hard to find that the person you love loves someone else. I knew that my tenure with Clarissa and Teddy would have an end.

It was early June, and I had continued my pattern with Teddy, and had continued to incrementally withdraw my attachment to Clarissa. There were other nights, nights involving quiet door closings and early morning slip-outs. These sounds made my detachment easier, even though there was no official announcement of a pledge of love, even though, as far as I knew, there was no introduction of the new man to Teddy, which I felt was wise of Clarissa and protective toward her child.

On a particularly disastrous afternoon I was in charge of Teddy and he and I engaged in a battle of wits. My mind was coherent, rational, cogent. His was not. As compelling as my arguments were, his nonverbal mind resisted. We had no unifying language or belief. I wanted a counselor to mediate, who would come and interpret for us, find common ground, a tenet we could agree on, then lead us into mutually agreed-on behavior. All this angst was focused on a cloth ring that fit over a cloth pole. He screamed, he wanted it, he didn't want

173

it, he cursed – I'm sure it was cursing – and there was absolutely no avenue for calm. But there were moments of transition. The moments of his transition from finding one thing unpleasant to finding another unpleasant. And he would gaze into my eyes, as if to read what I wanted from him so he could do the opposite. But these transitions were also moments of stillness, and in stillness is when my mind churns the fastest. I looked into the wells of his irises, into the murky pools of the lenses that zeroed in and out.

I had spent time with him; I had been the face, on occasion, that he woke up to. I was fixed in him; my image was held in his consciousness, and I wondered if his recollection of me had slipped beneath the watermark of his awareness and entered into a dreamy primordial place. I wondered if he saw me as his father. If he did, everything made sense. I was the safe one, the one he could rage against. The one from whom he would learn the nature, the limitation, and the context of the cloth ring on the cloth pole.

I constructed a triangle in my head. At its base was Teddy's identification of me as hero, along its ascending sides ran my participation in Teddy's life, however brief that participation might prove to be. At the apex was the word 'triumph,' and its definition spewed out of the triangle like a Roman candle: If one day Teddy, the boy and child, approached me with trust, if one morning he ran to my bedroom to wake me, if one afternoon he was happy to see me and bore a belief that I would not harm him, then I would have achieved victory over my past.

But my thoughts did not mollify Teddy; he wanted action. It was now dusk and he continued to orate in soprano screams. I decided a trip to the Rite Aid was in order, and he softened his volume when I swept him up and indicated we were on our way outside.

The sky over the ocean was lit with incandescent streaks of maroon. The air hinted that the evening would be warm, as nothing moved, not a leaf. Teddy, a strong walker now, put his hand up for me to take, and I hunched over and walked at old-man speed. We walked along the sidewalk and I occasionally would playfully swing him over an impending crack. I approached the curb, where I normally would have turned left and headed eight driveways down to where I could cross the street. But I paused.

My hand smothered Teddy's. I looked at him and knew that after my cohabitation with Clarissa was over, he might not remember me at all. Yet I knew I was influencing him. Every smile or frown I sent his way was registering, every raised voice or gentle praise was logged in his spongy mind. I wondered if what I wanted to pass along to him was my convoluted route to the Rite Aid, born of fear and nonsense, if what I wanted him to take from me was my immobility and panic as I faced an eight-inch curb. Or would I do for him what Brian had done for me? Would I lead him, as Brian had me, across the fearful place and would I let him hold on to me as I had held on to Brian? Suddenly, turning left toward my maze of driveways was as impossible as stepping off the curb. I could not leave Teddy with a legacy of fear from an unremembered place. I pulled him toward the curb so he would not be like me. Recalling the day I flew over it with a running leap, I put out one foot into the street, so he would not be like me. He effortlessly stepped off, swaying with stiff knees. I checked the traffic and we started forth. I walked him across the street so that he would not be like me. I led him up on the curb. I continued my beeline to the Rite Aid, a route I had only imagined existed. Across streets, down sidewalks, in crosswalks and out of them, all so Teddy would not be like me. I was the *Santa Maria* and Teddy was the *Niña* and *Pinta*. I led, he followed. I conquered each curb and blazed a new route south and achieved the Rite Aid in fifteen minutes.

As I entered the store, I did not feel any elation; in fact, it was as if my triumph had never happened. I felt that this was the way things were supposed to be, and I sensed that my curb fear had been an indulgence so that I might feel special. I let Teddy's hand go and he shifted into cruise. I followed him down the aisle, sometimes urging him along, once stopping him from sweeping down an entire display of bath soaps. I did not, however, prevent him cascading an entire bottom row of men's hair coloring onto the floor.

I sat Teddy down and tried to group the dyes in

their previous order. Men's medium brown, men's dark brown, men's ash blond. Men's mustache brown gel. A woman's arm extended into the mess and picked one up. Her skin was exposed at the wrist because her lab coat pulled back as she reached. She wore a small chrome watch and a delicately filigreed silver bracelet, so light it made no noise as it moved. As her arm reached into my vision, I heard her say, 'Is he yours?'

I looked up and saw Zandy, who was a full aisle's length away from her pharmacy post, and I wondered if she had intentionally walked toward us or was just passing by.

'No, he belongs to a friend.'

'What's his name?' she said.

'Teddy.'

'Hello, little man,' she said. Then she turned to me, 'I fill your prescriptions here sometimes, so I know all your maladies. My name's Zandy.'

I knew her name and she knew mine, but I told her again, including my middle name, and she cocked her head an inch to the sky. We had now gotten all the hair dye back on the shelf, and Zandy stood while I crouched on the ground wrangling Teddy. Zandy wore panty hose that were translucent with a wash of white, and she had on running shoes that I assumed were to cushion her feet against the concrete floors of the Rite Aid. While I took in her feet and legs, her voice fell on me from above:

'Would you like to get a pizza?'

Teddy and I, led by Zandy, walked around the

corner to Café Delores and ordered a triple something with a thin crust. I looked at Zandy and thought
that she occupied her own space rather nicely. I
thought of the status of my love life, which was as
flaky as the coming pizza. I knew it was time. I
decided to summon the full power of my charisma
and unleash it on this pharmacist. But nothing
came. It seemed there was no need because Zandy
was in full charge of herself and didn't need anything
extra to determine what she thought about me. I
said, 'How long have you worked at the pharmacy?'
But instead of answering, she smiled, then laughed
and put her hand on mine, and said, 'Oh, you don't
have to make conversation. I already like you.'

Zandy Alice Allen proved to be the love of my life.
I asked her once why she started talking to me
that day and she said, 'It was the way you were
with the boy.' After seeing her for several weeks,
I recalled Clarissa's front-door kiss. I emulated her
seducer and one night at Zandy's doorstep, pressed
her against me. Her head fell back and I kissed
her. Her arms dropped to her side, then after a
moment of helplessness, she raised her hands and
held my arms. She drew in a breath while my lips
were on hers, and I think she whispered the word
'love,' but it was obscured by my mouth on hers.
    Once we were at lunch and she asked how old
I was and I told her the truth: thirty-one. Months
went by and she got to the heart of me. With a
cheery delicacy she divided my obsessions into

three categories: acceptable, unacceptable, and hilarious. The unacceptable ones were those that inhibited life, like the curbs. But Teddy had already successfully curtailed that one; each time I approached a corner, I envisioned myself as a leader and in time the impulse vanished. The other intolerable ones she simply vetoed, and I was able to adjourn them, or convert them into a mistrust of icebergs. The tolerable ones included silent counting and alphabetizing, though when Angela arrived she left me little time to indulge myself. We compromised on the lights, but eventually Zandy's humor – which included suddenly flicking lamps on and off and then dashing out of the room – made the obsession too unnerving to indulge in.

It took six months and a wellspring of perseverance for me to stop the government checks from coming in. I was able to go back to work for Hewlett-Packard and I moved up the ladder when I created a cipher so human that no computer could crack it. Zandy and I lived at the Rose Crest after Clarissa left, though she and Teddy stayed in our lives until one day they just weren't anymore. I knew that what happened between Teddy and me would one day be revealed to him. One night Zandy and I were in bed and she leaned over to me and whispered that she was pregnant, and I pulled her into me and we entwined ourselves and made slow and silent love without breaking our gaze to one another.

Angela was born on April 5, 2003, which pleased me because her twenty-first brithday would fall on a Friday, which meant she would be able to sleep late the next day after what would undoubtedly be a late night of partying.

When Angela was one year old, Zandy took her out to a small birthday fete for little ladies only and I was left alone at the Rose Crest. From the window I could see my old apartment and see my old lamp just through the curtains. This was the lamp I had once dressed in my shirt and used as a stand-in to determine whether Elizabeth could have seen me look at her, and now at the Rose Crest I felt far, far away from that moment. I indulged myself in one old pastime. As I looked across the street, I built in my head my final magic square:

Me	Zandy's mom, Sandy	Our neighbor, Mrs. Thompson, who loves Angela
Philipa	Zandy and Angela	Brian
Granny's Memory	Clarissa and Teddy	My sister, Ida

Other names came, but the square overflowed and the confusion pleased me. I shifted away from the window, turning my back on the apartment across the street. I moved to the living room and sat, silently thanking those who had brought me here and those who had affected me, both above and below consciousness. I thought of the names in and around the magic square. I thought of their astounding number, both in the present and past, of Zandy and Angela, of Brian, of Granny, even of my father, whose disavowal of me led to this place, and I understood that as much as I had resisted the outside, as much as I had constricted my life, as much as I had closed and narrowed the channels into me, there were still many takers for the quiet heart.

ACKNOWLEDGMENTS

I would like to thank my diligent and inspiring editor, Leigh Haber, as well as my conscripted friends who were forced to read various drafts and held in a cellar until they offered in-depth commentary: Sarah Paley, Carol Muske-Dukes, Deborah Solomon, Sherle and John, Victoria Dailey, Susan Wheeler, April and Eric and Mary Karr. I would also like to thank Ricky Jay, who in minutes assembled a short treatise for my enlightenment on magic squares from his own amazing library. And Duke.